"I read this book in one day. I could not put it down."
~ Jack Martin Mcdonald Jr.

"Amazing book! I love it! The plot is really interesting and uent. The characters are sympathetic and
the intimate moments steamy. All in all an amazing
read and highly recommended."

The Find of Her Life

Anna Patten
&
Tim LaSure

Copyright © 2016 by Anna Patten & Tim LaSure

Printed in the United States of America
Edited by: Amanda Marie
Cover Design: Linkville Graphics

Linkville Press
linkvillepress.com
linkvillepress@gmail.com

ISBN-13: 978-1-947794-09-2
ISBN-10: 1-947794-09-4

A portion of all proceeds goes to Villalobos Rescue Center.
vrcpitbull.com

Dedicated with gratitude and love to those who would not allow me to give up on this project. You held my hand, lent your shoulders, and talked me down when I was sure I could not go on. For that I will be forever grateful.
~ Anna

To all people who's souls always make room for more life.
~ Tim

Prologue

MEXICO
NOVEMBER

"Senorita Macleod!" The shout came from across the dig site. "Senorita Macleod!" It came again, this time more insistent.

Maggie dropped her brush and looked up into the afternoon sunlight. She raised her hand to shield her eyes from the hot Mexican sun. There was not a breeze in sight and she knew the heat would be unbearable in a few hours. She was irritated at this interruption. Arriving late to the site, she had barely begun to work, and now this.

Maggie smiled to herself, feeling a faint hint of a blush coming on. She had been late getting to the site because Michael would not let her out of bed. He had insisted on making love for the second time that morning, even though they were on a deadline. She took a deep breath, pushing back a few locks of auburn hair that had escaped from under her hat. Her mind wandered. This was to be the last dig before she and Michael headed home to get married. An event she had been waiting two years for.

The museum had kept them busy for most of that time. They had accepted this assignment because of reassurances that this was an important dig. She had to admit, Mexico was one of her favorite places on Earth. It was always warm and full of beautiful beaches. On the rare occasions that she and Michael got time off, they always went there. The past month had been blissful for them, even though the two of them rarely got to work together. The fact that it came so close to their wedding made it all the more special to her.

Maggie pulled herself up the ladder and out of the pit she was in, only to find a flood of workers running towards her.

"Señorita Macleod!" the call came again.

She took off her hat and ran towards them. Now what? she wondered.

Maggie reached the first worker and saw the look of fright on his face. "What is it, José?"

"Señorita!" he gasped, his eyes wild with fright. "Come quick! Señor Tucker...he has been hurt!" Maggie felt her heart drop, fear gripping her.

Her feet began to move, seemingly of their own volition, before the thought had come to her to run. "Michael!" she screamed. She ran across the desert floor, feeling that the dig site grew with every step. The sun felt like an oppressive weight on her. "Michael!" she screamed again.

In the distance she could see people standing around the largest pit with shovels. A few were digging already. She came to them and fell to her knees. Maggie felt tears warm on her face as she surveyed the now covered pit. The only thing she could see was Michael's hand sticking up out of the mound of dirt. She reached for it and clasped it tightly.

"Michael!" She felt him grip her hand. "Hold on, Michael! We are going to get you out of there! Hold on!" She looked around at everyone. "Dig faster!" she shouted.

Maggie felt Michael's hand slip and she reached blindly for it. "I've got you, Baby! Pull yourself up! Don't quit on me, Michael! Please!"

She felt his hand slip again until his fingers were completely out of her grasp and under the dirt. To her horror, the walls of the pit caved inward. "Michael, don't leave me!" She dug wildly with her hands. "Michael!"

DOLA, WEST VIRGINIA
MAY

"O-si-yo," Ben said, coming to the edge of the mowed area in front of his grandfather's house.

"Sahale!" His grandfather laughed with joy, rising to his feet. His hands and knees were muddy from the dozen tomato plants he had just set in the ground.

"Where did you get the tomato plants?" Ben asked, looking them over and grabbing the nozzle of a nearby water hose.

"From the FFA. I always help the kids out. You know they stop and talk to me when they go up the holler here. They're good kids, I think."

"Yeah, well, one of these days the cops will find what they're growing up there." Ben laughed, gently spraying water on the fragile tomato plants.

"They did not find yours." His grandfather chuckled. "No, they are good kids; they walk up the holler, instead of riding up it on a four-wheeler. They respect my wishes and I help them out. Here, I need a drink." He took the hose from Ben and pressed the nozzle close to his lips. The water dribbled down his weathered chin and soaked his denim shirt.

John Adams was in his late 70s, with long grey hair peppered slightly with the jet black of his youth. Looking at him one might want to offer him a chair, but most people would take a break well before him were they to take a walk up the hillside that seemed

4

The Find of Her Life Anna Patten/Tim Lasure

to shove his house closer to the creek each year. He paused with a distant look, as if carefully composing before each sentence, yet there was little doubt his mind was sharp. Ben followed, walking to the edge of the porch and sitting down. "You headed somewhere?"

"I was going to Clarksburg to get some...things," Ben said, catching himself.

"Parts for that four-wheeler?"

"Okay, yeah, something like that." Ben laughed, lowering his head in embarrassment.

"It's good that you stopped. You know, Joseph took me to the meeting last week and I wanted to tell you about it."

"How is Uncle Joe?" Ben asked. His tone indicated politeness more than curiosity. Ben was social with his uncle, but rarely saw him once he finished college.

"He is fine. You know he has a new truck, much like yours, but fancier I think," his grandfather said, moving his hands in an effort to enhance the description. "I did not tell him, but I had a vision the night before the meeting."

Ben was now listening attentively. He could recall being told that his grandfather had two other visions in his life. One was of the birth of a child in their family, in which he mapped out the child's successes with scary accuracy right through high school. The other vision was when Ben was a year old and his parents lived in Buffalo Creek, West Virginia.

John saw his oldest son and daughter-in-law "swallowed by a black wall." Two days later, at 7:15 AM, February 6, 1972, Ben's mother had taken him to his Uncle Joseph's house to stay while she cleaned for some wealthier families in the area. An hour later, a twenty-foot high wall of mud and water fully engulfed both the house she was working in and their family home when an earth dam built recklessly by a coal company broke. One hundred eighteen people were killed, including both of his parents.

"A vision?"

"Yes. I saw you stray from your path, which has been a good path. I think this new path is a good one also, even though there are many others there before you. When you decided you had traveled this new path far enough, you turned to go back, but a deer stood in your way. You were cautious, as I taught you, until you noticed the deer was in trouble...dying in its suffering. This deer did not look at you, but you recognized its hurt. You cared for it, and in your caring the deer found strength, and this made you happy, and so you followed it more. Watching it made you know you had done a good thing. This deer...it leads you where you never thought to go, but in the end you were happy, as you found something that had been lost...on this path. I could not see what it was, but it was good. It was good for you and the people.

You heard the deer cry out for you again, and you knew it was in great danger, maybe injured. You did not know whether to follow, because in the other direction were the voices of a thousand human beings. This is for you to decide." He then got a far away look in his eye and stared across the field, the wind blowing the season's first grass.

"Is that it?"

"Yes. I think it means sometimes we see a great thing before us, but have a choice to make."

"Grandpa, that just sounds like a dream. There's nothing I can take from it, or am I missing something?"

"What we see is a drop in the river of what we miss. I am sure in the future it will be clear. I wanted to tell you this, and ask a favor. I ask you this for the people," the old man said, repositioning himself on the wooden edge of the porch. "At the meeting we talked about the new four-lane they are building on the Ohio."

"Yeah, Route 2, it's going to eventually run from Chester to Huntington."

"Some of the people, they remember stories of our ancestors, about the Ohio River. It was good there, you know?"

"Oh...I would imagine our people were all over the Ohio Valley at one time, Grandpa," Ben said, standing and stretching his back.

"It would be a good thing then if you would watch over our land, before the new road is built. Some of it runs near the school where you teach. Others have done this for the people, and found burial grounds and things. They were able to preserve the rights of our ancestors before the new road came. This is what we ask."

Ben thought for a moment and realized it was very important to his grandfather, as well as other Native Americans, that he accept this request. However, the truth was that he had not been actively involved in Native American affairs of late, and wondered if he were the best choice. "Well, you know, Grandpa, I'll do everything I can, but I'm not sure how to go about this," he said, watching the old man's face closely.

"We contacted a man in Charleston. Here is his number," he said, taking a piece of paper from his shirt pocket. "Call him and tell him the Cherokee people want you to represent their interests. Then call me and let me know how things go."

"Yeah, well that's one thing I wanted to talk to you about. Do you ever answer your phone?"

"Don't you remember? You bought me the phone with answering machine, so that I would not have to."

Ben fought off a laugh, saying, "Grandpa that is so that when you're not here you'll not miss any calls, not to handle your calls when you're sitting there by the phone."

The old man walked back to his tomato plants, shaking his head, and said, "Do you always give gifts and then tell people how to use them? I thought it was a good idea. I can even hear your voice and listen to it again if I forget." "How many tomato plants did you get? Are you going to be able to keep up with these all summer?"

He considered this for a time, then picked up a hoe and dug into the soil, before asking, "Do you remember what I told you? White man builds a big fire and sits way back."

"That's right, Grandpa, and this sure looks like a bigger fire than you need. To me anyway."

"Well...one more thing I will tell you," he said, turning and pointing a finger toward Ben's nose, "those tomatoes from the stores suck!"

"Yep, they sure do, Grandpa," Ben chuckled.

"I'm going to can these...or something! I'm not buying tomatoes next winter. Taste more like socks."

"All right, Grandpa," Ben said with a laugh. "I got to get going, but I wanted to stop and say hi and leave you some cash. I'll just put it on the table, okay?"

"Okay, and call that man tonight."

"I will, Grandpa," Ben said, walking on the porch and entering the house.

"And if you get his answering machine, just leave a message. He'll hear it eventually."

Ben chuckled to himself. He walked across the room and put an envelope on the table. He then looked around the room for signs of how his grandfather was doing. Dishes in the sink indicated he had breakfast, and a quick check of the refrigerator told him he was set with food. The place was at least as clean as Ben's own house. Beside his recliner was a coffee table with the phone on top of two old phone books, just an arm's length away. He smiled and walked outside.

"Have fun on that four-wheeler," his grandfather yelled to him as he walked across the lawn, and then under his breath, "can't wait to see gasoline go to $5 a gallon. Maybe $10!"

Chapter 1

WASHINGTON DC
MAY

The morning sun was shining brightly through the heavily pained windows of the conservatory. The East Coast was enjoying an unseasonably warm spring, and as Maggie looked out, she could see the throngs of early vacationers enjoying the day. Maggie watched them intently, wishing that she could feel an ounce of the happiness that they did.

She caught a glimpse of him emerging from the cherry trees that lined the walkway before cutting across the lawn, as he had so many times before. A smile came to her lips as she took in the sight of him. Tall and lean, his blond hair shining in the sunlight. As if he sensed her, he looked up and smiled. Maggie placed her hand against the glass of the window. "Michael," she whispered. She watched him take his glasses off to clean them. Those damned glasses! she thought. Oh, how he had been resistant to change, preferring to keep the old wire-rimmed glasses instead of contacts.

"Maggie," the voice called.

Maggie closed her eyes, trying to remember every detail of his face, knowing that this memory she had conjured up would not be there when she opened them again.

"Maggie," the voice called again.

She felt a hand touch her shoulder and she opened her green eyes. A single tear escaped and slipped down her cheek. Reaching up, Maggie quickly dried it and turned towards the touch. Warm brown eyes greeted her.

"Maggie," Bev said, "it's so good to see you."

"It's good to see you too, old friend," Maggie replied. Pulling back, she took in the sight of the woman in front of her.

Beverly Altman had been her friend for as long as she could remember. They met on a dig when Maggie was just a child on summer vacation. She had decided that the only place she wanted to spend her summer vacation that year was in the dirt with her dad. Later, Bev, a well-established archeologist herself, was one of her college professors at Boston University. Now, so many years later, she was her boss at the Smithsonian, but most important to Maggie was the fact that Bev was her friend.

It always amazed her how Bev never seemed to age. At sixty, she was still one of the most beautiful women Maggie had ever known—all five feet of her. There before her stood a firecracker of a woman who took a hammer to the glass ceiling for women in the field of archeology.

Bev smoothed her dark hair back. "I must look a mess. I've been in meetings all morning," she said with a laugh. "You look beautiful, as always." Bev smiled and reached for Maggie's hand.

"Let's walk." Maggie agreed and they walked down the long hallway of the conservatory. "How are you, Kid?" Bev asked with concern. "I wish everyone would stop asking me that!

I'm fine." "Well, you look like hell."

Maggie stopped and turned towards her friend. "Is this why I came here today?" she asked, her anger flaring.

"No, I dare say not. You came here today to ask me to send you back to work. Telling you 'no' on the phone didn't register with you apparently."

"I need to go back to work!"

Bev reached up and took her by the shoulders. "What you need is to grieve, Margaret."

Maggie looked away, trying to hold back a flood of tears. She didn't want to grieve. If she did, that would mean that he was truly gone—a realization that she was not ready to face yet. She turned and met the scrutiny of Bev's gaze again. Knowing her green eyes were glassy.

"Bev, I cannot go back to Ma's. I know she means well, but she is driving me crazy. She has Collin calling me every day. I'm sure she would have Charlie and Trevor follow suit, but they're out in the field."

"You are lucky to have brothers who care about you, Honey."

"It's too much!" Maggie fought to control her emotion.

Bev took her hand and they walked again. "And your father? If anyone understands you, surely it's him."

Maggie smiled at the thought of that. She and her dad had always been close. He always knew the right things to say. "Dad's in Europe right now. He stayed home as long as he could. He begged me to go with him and I would have..."

"If you would not have gone behind my back and had Roger send you to Chile."

"I have to work, Bev, so I can breathe! You wouldn't send me anywhere. I wasn't gone nearly long enough either," Maggie pleaded.

"Well, I can see that we will have to do this the hard way. Since you won't listen to your friends or family, and since you did go behind my back, you leave me with no other choice. Be in New Martinsville, West Virginia in two days."

"West Virginia? Surely you..."

"I assure you I'm not joking! This dig is beneath you, I know that, but somebody has to do it and since you're so eager to run away from everything, you can have it."

Maggie felt her anger flare again. "You think by offering me a lame assignment, you will get me to stay home? This is one of my mother's tactics."

"Rachel is a good teacher," Bev said with a smile, "and I'm thinking no such thing. You want to work and this is what I have to offer right now."

"What about Greece?"

"That's on the back burner for now. Take it or leave it, Mags."

They had come to Bev's office door and Maggie threw it open, stalking inside. She flopped down in the large leather armchair in front of the desk and took a deep breath. She looked around and fought the urge to smile. Bev's office had always been a wonderful place for her. It was like going to the circus. Artifacts from far and wide lined her mahogany shelves, and pictures of her on various digs hung on the wall. Maggie reached over, picked up the skull that always sat on Bev's desk, and held it tightly in her hands. When she was a child and they would come to the museum with her father, her brothers would always abandon her. They went off on some "boy's only" adventure and she always wound up in here. The skull had been a friend of sorts and she found it very comforting to hold now.

"Honey, I know you think I'm playing hardball with you…"

"You are, aren't you?"

"No," Bev said, closing the office door behind her. She walked around the large oak desk and sat down in the other large leather chair opposite Maggie. "This could actually be an exciting dig."

"Bev, you know as well as I do that nothing has ever been found in the burial mounds out there. They were all looted."

"Well, you're not going to the burial mounds. The state has been doing some roadwork up there. They're trying to widen the highway or something. Anyway, they've stumbled onto some Native American artifacts and they've asked us to come in."

"You're sending me out there for arrowheads?" Maggie asked, somewhat insulted.

"Not just arrowheads, Mags. They've found some interesting objects. Now, I've grown tired of your attitude! Take it or leave it!"

Maggie took a deep breath and looked out the window. It's either this or Ma's, she thought. Ma hovering over her was a thought that pained her. She felt defiant and met her friend's eyes. "Fine. I'll be there."

Bev smiled and reached for an envelope lying on her desk. She handed it to Maggie. "Everything you need is in there. Oh, and there's one catch."

Maggie snatched the envelope out of her hand begrudgingly. "Of course there is," she said sarcastically.

"The Elder Council of the ANAWV is sending a representative out to work with you. You're to show him every kindness, is that understood?"

"Is he a digger?" "No, he's a professor." "Great! Just what I need, an amateur," Maggie said under her breath.

"Every kindness, Mags! Do not embarrass me, or the museum."

Maggie stood up, clutching the envelope in her hands. "Fine, I will work with him, but he better not get in my way." She met her friend's eyes, feeling emotional. "Thank you, Bev," she said in a hushed voice, placing the skull back on the desk.

Bev got up and put her arms around her friend tightly. "If you need anything, you call me." She pulled back, holding Maggie's shoulders. "You hear? Anything!"

Maggie nodded in agreement and turned to go. She walked through the museum towards the sunlight and felt panicked. She had to go home and tell Ma the news. That was a prospect that would scare anyone.

Chapter 2

*T*he night sky was clear and lit with stars. Sitting down on the big porch swing, Maggie prayed that it would not creek and give away her location. Her mind had not yet formulated the method in which she would tell her mother she was leaving again. The flight from Dulles had been flawlessly easy. She had landed just after rush hour, so the drive home had been equally as nice. Now came the hard part.

The cool night air put her at ease and Maggie closed her eyes. How she loved nights like this. Why is this so hard? she thought. It was hard because her mother had guarded her like a pitbull for the last six months. Her whole life, really. It was tough being the only girl in a rough and tumble family such as hers. Ma was always there for her.

She took a deep breath and looked up at the stars. A memory of Mexico flashed into her mind and Maggie fought the urge to cry out. As if sensing her daughter's pain, the screen door opened and her mother stuck her head out.

"Margaret, is that you?" Her mother's Scottish accent floated out on the breeze.

Maggie rolled her eyes. "Yes, Ma, I'm back." Her mother's slight frame came into view.

Rachel Macleod was a perfect lady in every sense of the word and her title only added to that. She very rarely ever wore pants. It just was not proper for a lady to do so. Fiercely proud of her family and proud to be a stay-at-home mom, Rachel had managed to raise four kids while their dad was out trekking the globe. She kept everything and everyone together when Robert decided to move the family from their home in Scotland to Boston. Rachel always made sure that their three-story home was a safe haven for the whole family. To this day her mother would tell anyone who would listen that when she saw Lord Robert Macleod, the Earl of Glencairn for the first time, she knew that she would love him forever. Robert, in turn would say that there had never been anyone in the world as beautiful as Rachel. With all of the scrapes her father had gotten into over the years, Maggie always thought them lucky that they had gotten to spend their lives together. A blessing she thought she would share with Michael. That was gone now.

Maggie fought the stirrings of overwhelming grief again and met her mother's green eyes.

"How was your trip?" Rachel questioned, sitting down next to her daughter. "How is Beverly?"

"Good. Bev sends her love."

Rachel reached over, clasping Maggie's hand tightly. "You're leaving again?"

How does she do that? Maggie wondered. Her mother always knew something before anyone told her. "Yes, Ma, but it's not far this time. Just West Virginia. My plane leaves tomorrow. Early afternoon." Rachel's grip tightened. "I know you think I hover over you, and maybe I do, but your da' and I are worried. There is no denying that you will face this, Maggie girl. When it finally hits you, I would have you with family. You can na' run forever."

Her mother's accent was always warm and comforting. Like a cozy blanket to wrap yourself in on a crisp fall night.

Maggie felt warm tears on her face. They always came as such a shock to her. There was never any warning. "I can na'! I can't do this! Not now!" Her own accent was coming out.

Rachel put her arm around her daughter and pulled her head back to rest on her shoulder. "Well then, my girl, I'd best help you pack. Promise me that you will call your da' and let him know where you are."

Maggie lifted her head and stared into her lovely eyes,

always struck by her mother's beauty. Her mother's brilliant red hair had begun to fade some, but her eyes were as green as emeralds and her skin as flawless as silk. She brought a hand to her mother's face and tried to smile. "I will, I promise, if you promise to call Collin off."

Rachel laughed, "You caught on to that, I see." She leaned in and kissed her daughter's forehead. "I will call him off."

"The truth be known, Ma, I would rather be going to Greece. Bev won't send me there." "So the phone call I made to her was helpful then. I asked her to keep ya close to home." Maggie pulled away and felt her anger flare. "Ma, you didn't! I told you I will deal with this in my own way."

"You are my daughter and I will do what I think is right. Greece is too far away and when this hits you, Margaret, I will have you close to family. That's the end of it. Now, come inside and have some supper. I will help you pack in the morning," Rachel said as she stood up.

Maggie watched her mother walk across the porch and inside the house before she let out a cry of frustration. She felt like pulling her hair out. It will be good to get to West Virginia, she thought, standing up.

Taking one last look at the night sky she made her way inside. The morning would not come soon enough.

Chapter 3

*M*aggie checked two bags at the skycap and rolled a carry-on and her briefcase into Logan International Airport's main terminal. It was crowded, even for early morning, so she put her cell on vibrate and in her pants' pocket in hopes of catching calls. Security was backed up, but her flight was an hour from departure, so she was not concerned about time.

Maggie stood in line people watching, as she often did when killing time in crowds. In front of her was a man talking on a Bluetooth to a coworker, wearing way too much cologne. Making the next turn in the tapes was a college-aged girl with a huge backpack, reading a book on scientology. Her hair was haphazardly braided and her canvas shoes soiled. As she read, she bumped into an elderly couple in front of her and apologized. The elderly couple wore matching tropical shirts. Maggie watched them study their itineraries, always smiling, sometimes whispering nose to nose. The image put a smile on Maggie's, wondering if they might be on a trip celebrating an anniversary. The smile faded quickly, thinking of the fantasies she had several months prior and how they had disappeared so abruptly.

After clearing security, Maggie sat down in a nearby chair to adjust her luggage. Her cell vibrated. She pulled the phone from her pocket and saw the name "Collin" on the screen.

"Hello, can you hear me? I'm at the airport," Maggie said in a raised voice.

"Hi. Yes, I can hear you just fine. So you're off again?" Collin replied.

"Yes, for a while." Maggie did not elaborate but examined the monitor above to see that her flight was still on time.

"Okay, well, I just wanted to catch you before you got busy. I'm still at the same number, you know."

Maggie rolled her eyes in an attempt to ward away the guilt and frustration. She hadn't been good about returning calls or even answering the phone for months. "I know, Collin. I'm sorry, I've just been a little busy, and nothing to report anyway."

"I'll take nothing as a report anytime. It's good to hear your voice. I've been busy working on a new project myself. You remember me telling you...well, okay, one of the waste products we deal with here is a derivative of hydrochloric acid, and it's not very easy to..."

"Collin, I'm sorry, but I have to board now. I want to hear about it, though. Can I call you tonight or tomorrow?" Maggie interrupted.

"Oh, I'm sorry. Yeah, no problem, sister of mine. I just wanted to say have a nice trip and stay in touch, okay?"

"Absolutely," Maggie said, heading for the terminal. "I should get to my hotel this afternoon, so maybe this evening I'll have the chance to call and we can talk."

"Sounds good," replied Collin. "Love you!"

"I love you, too. Bye." Maggie put the phone back in her pocket.

The flight was bumpy but brief and Maggie was relieved when the plane dropped below 10,000 feet through a low cloud cover on its approach. She exited the jet way, stepping inside Pittsburgh International at 11:20 AM. By the time her two checked bags made the carousel she was feeling a bit hungry, which only added to her struggle to the car rental counter where she secured a Suburban for a month. It seemed such a long time period to her now and she fantasized about the day she would return the vehicle and see home again.

As the shuttle took her to her Suburban, it started to rain and she had to quickly put her bags in the back. Her hair and clothes were somewhat wet by the time she was in the vehicle, which made her decide to not stop on the way, but wait to eat later after checking into her hotel.

After checking a map to get her bearings, she pulled out of the lot and was soon on the busy interstate. She headed west through Pennsylvania toward the northern panhandle of West Virginia. Traffic was heavy, but nothing compared to Boston, and she whipped the big SUV into the passing lane time and time again through the rain, making excellent time. As she neared the state line, the hills became steeper and longer. Low clouds hanging just above the rising fog emitted a constant drizzle that made her sleepy, yet she managed to stay alert, familiarizing herself with the surroundings. The landscape became lush with tall, close trees even along the interstate. It was dreary and dark for the middle of the day, but the scenery was not unpleasant.

Finally she saw a sign ahead that read, "Sistersville," and she dropped down a hill and into a small town. Houses, churches, and a few businesses lay close to the narrowing highway and the speed limit seemed unnecessarily slow to her. She looked for the quaint Victorian Inn she had found online as the main road twisted at odd angles through the town. When her final destination, The Dogwood Inn, became visible on her right she gave out a sigh of relief.

She parked in a lot across the street, grabbed one bag, her briefcase, and stepped out of the Suburban just as the rain increased to a downpour. Her clothes were again soaked by the time she made the door and walked inside the dimly lit lobby. Looking around, she smiled, seeing just what she had hoped the place would be. Wide doorways were lined with ornate woodwork. Beautiful chairs, as well as tables and brightly adorned period pieces sat on tasteful carpeting; not at all like the boring and loud chain-type hotels. Down one hall she could see a gift shop that she knew she would be visiting, whereas in the opposite corner a glass case stood displaying books about the history of the area.

"Miss Macleod?" a voice called from across the room. Maggie looked to see an older man, tall, very thin, wearing black pants, white shirt, and suspenders. He had a bald head, round wire-rimmed glasses, and a very long, full, grey beard.

"Yes," Maggie answered, stepping toward him and offering her hand.

"I've been watching for you. Hope the rain didn't give ya any trouble?"

He reached to shake her hand and help her with her bag, then lead her to the front desk. "I'm Troy Higgins. Your room is ready. You should have a good wireless Internet signal in there, and I put today's paper on the desk for ya."

"Oh...wonderful," said Maggie, searching her purse and laying a credit card on the desk. "The drive was not a problem, just got a little wet." She looked to see her USA Today was soaking wet and threw it in a nearby wastebasket.

"I have you down for...twenty eight nights, is that right?"

"Yes, for now. Will I be able to keep that room longer if needed?"

"That should be no problem," said Troy. "Back yonder is our restaurant and it's open from 11 AM till 9 PM. We have a pub, pool, hot tub, a real nice new workout center...and I think that's it. Like I said, my name's Troy, and just call me if you need anything. We're awfully glad to have you here. Here's a key, and I can help you with your other bags, if you have any." Troy stepped out from behind the desk and looked out the door.

Maggie walked toward the door and commented, "I think I have all I need right now. Maybe when it stops raining I'll get the rest of it." She grabbed the key off the desk, asking, "Room 202?"

"Yes, ma'am," Troy said, pointing. "Right at the top of the steps on your right."

Maggie made her way up to the second floor, opened the door to her room, removed her shoes, and placed her briefcase on the couch. The room was decorated in shades of pink, and looked so cozy to her. The furnishings looked late 19th century. On every tabletop and in every corner were knickknacks, making the room seem more like a home than a temporary habitation. There was a sitting area with a TV, while across the room she noticed a sleigh bed with several pillows that she could not resist another second. She flopped down on the bed, closed her eyes, and listened to the sound of the rain running down gutters and tapping against the glass of the window. Her intention was to shower, make some phone calls, then get online to do some research, but that would have to be postponed. Exhausted from her travels, she gave into her weariness and drifted off to sleep before she knew it.

However, after an hour of tossing and turning she decided to get up. The clock on the nightstand read 3 PM, so she figured it was time to unpack a few items, and headed for the shower. The water took a long time to get warm, but once there, she felt it soothe her bones and her spirit. Maggie would have stayed under the water longer, but her hunger got the best of her, so she reluctantly shut it off.

After her shower, she put on a pair of khaki shorts and a blouse before sitting on the edge of the bed to put on her shoes. She drew back the pink sheers and looked out the window. It had stopped raining and was somewhat brighter out. Where are the people? she thought, looking directly below. The only signs of life were at the convenience store up the block. Hopefully that would be a handy place. She then took the newspaper from the desk and headed down to the restaurant.

Entering the restaurant, Maggie wondered if she was in the right place. There were two dining rooms, one larger and more formal. Finally she saw a lady emerge from the kitchen, wiping her hands on an apron that she wore over a white blouse and black pants. Maggie must have looked somewhat bewildered to her as she stood smiling and looking around the room.

"Oh, just sit anywhere you like, ma'am," the lady said, grabbing a menu and following Maggie to a table beside a window. "Can I get you something to drink?"

"Iced tea?" Maggie asked, looking over the menu. "Okay, iced tea, and do you need a few minutes to decide?"

"Umm, no, I'd like the chicken salad...and ranch dressing on the side, please," Maggie replied, handing the menu back to her.

"Okay," the waitress said cheerfully and headed back into the kitchen.

Maggie looked out the window to see a small courtyard that was landscaped in mostly perennial plants, with a few geraniums in clay pots. She then unfolded the paper. The Wetzel Chronicle, she read quietly. "Let's see what the big news items are. 'Two indicted on drug charges, twenty marijuana plants were destroyed after...' Yeah, big news there!'" Maggie chuckled, looking at some of the other news items. There were seven obituaries. Either there are not many people living around here, or the ones that are, are very healthy, she thought.

After devouring her lunch, Maggie returned to her room and took her laptop from her briefcase. She then went online to look at sites with information on the Native American people who once inhabited the Ohio Valley. One site in particular was about the Adena people, who built the ancient burial mound she had seen earlier that day. She read:

> The Adena people were the first Native Americans to build ceremonial mounds... We know little about how or why the mounds were built...but that they built them over the remains of chiefs, shamans, and priests...as early as 2000 BC... Mound builders everyday tools and products gave archaeologists a lot of information...knives, drills, picks, spears, axes, and projectile points. They obtained copper and pounded it into ornaments. Their pottery was the strongest of its time...

So, tools and pottery might be easy to find, she thought. After some reading she decided that there might be some opportunities here. Surely a culture that honored the dead with such a great effort for the time would have other impressive accomplishments, and maybe she would be the one to rediscover them. Pots and arrowheads made for good museum displays, but Maggie was always alert to find other parts of the lives of the cultures she studied. How the people enjoyed art, feared gods, lived and loved, were of more interest to her. She decided to apply her best tool— her passion for her work—to this effort.

Over the next few hours she moved chronologically through the history of other cultures and tribes of the Ohio Valley—Hopewell, Delaware Shawnee, Cherokee, the list was overwhelming. Things came to an end for them after the Revolutionary War, when most tribes moved westward. Plannning her investigation, Maggie took notes on how to handle samples for carbon dating and other tests. It was just enough to spur her curiosity.

Later her inability to see letters on the keyboard alerted Maggie that she had been at it for hours. Turning her gaze towards the windows, she noticed it had become dark outside. While not famished, the thought occurred to her to head downstairs for a bite; maybe just dessert or something would be nice. This time there was one other occupied table. A young couple sat nervously across from one another, occasionally touching hands. The blush of new love was written all over them and she smiled to herself. Oh how she could remember that feeling. The unexpected excitement that was yet to come. It made everything in the world better, well hers anyway. Then it hit her. She felt the pain and regret of her loss deep in her bones. When would that ever go away? she wondered. Maggie picked at her plate a bit, ate quickly, and returned to her room.

She entered the dark room and found her way to a light switch by the glow cast from street lights below. The rest of the luggage can wait until morning, but... she thought. Heaving a heavy sigh, she rifled through what was left in the suitcase, until she finally found what she was looking for. It was a metal, 5x7 frame surrounding a photo of her wearing a bathing suit on a beach in Mexico; she was being raised in the air by her three brothers and Michael. She held it in her hands and studied it as if she had never seen it before. Her thumb gently stroking the glass, she leaned her head back, and allowed tears to roll down her cheeks and onto her neck. Clutching the picture to her chest, she fell back on the bed. Rain beat the panes of glass in her room, the down pour growing stronger like the tears she shed when Michael died. A wind made a lonesome noise that only added to her feeling of hopelessness. Sometime between then and morning she managed to turn off the light, undress, and find a few hours of sleep.

Chapter 4

The alarm on Maggie's cell phone woke her at 6 AM. Opening her eyes, her senses were assaulted by the harsh morning light peeking through the curtains. She sighed heavily, inching out of bed, and slowly made her way to the window to look outside. The sky was mostly clear with a few clouds, still purple, before the sun had its chance to make it over the lush green hills. What a beautiful vista! Today will be a gorgeous day, Maggie mused. She yawned, stretched, then rubbed the sleep from her eyes. After a few moments of enjoying the morning sky, Maggie turned around to rifle through her bag. She found her day planner and opened it to confirm the location of her meeting with engineers from the state. New Martinsville. Maybe I should ask Troy to point me in the right direction, she contemplated while heading into the bathroom.

She turned the shower on and after a few moments stepped in. The water felt glorious as it rained down on her. Unfortunately she didn't have the time to linger since her meeting was to be at 8 am. She turned the water off, then stepped out to dry herself. Today will be warm, I think. Perfect! Opening her suitcase she found her shorts right on top. She hurriedly got dressed, then put her clothes into the dresser, before grabbing her gear and heading downstairs.

Troy was sweeping the lobby when Maggie approached. He smiled in greeting. "Good morning, Miss Macleod. Did ya have a good night?" he asked, straightening himself. He propped the broom against a corner and opened the front door for her.

"Good morning. I certainly did, thank you, Troy. Do you know where the state road office is at in New Martinsville?"

"Yes, ma'am. It's right along Route 2, on your right as you head north from here. Probably takes you about…thirty minutes to get there."

"Well, thank you. Also, I'm expecting a few packages to be delivered to me today," Maggie said, continuing towards the door.

"I'll be on the lookout for them. You have a good day now, Miss," she heard Troy call after her while passed him.

Stepping outside, she looked up at the crisp morning sky and inhaled deeply. Clean, fresh air filled her lungs; expelling the anxiety she felt the night before. Motivated by the beautiful morning and Troy's kind smile she headed to the parking lot. Digging in her pack for her car keys, she opened the driver side and climbed into the Suburban. Turning the vehicle on, she turned on her radio. Freddie Mercury's powerful voice sounded from the speakers. Maggie started to sing along with him as he sung under pressure. A sentiment that she could really identify with at the moment. She turned out of the parking lot and onto the highway, heading north.

Twenty-five minutes later she saw the West Virginia Department of Highways building on her right, and being half an hour early, she turned around to back-track through a drive-through she had passed earlier for a quick breakfast.

A breakfast sandwich and a cup of coffee were hardly the healthiest choices, but she had long gotten used to the primitive morning meals on the go. A painful memory flashed into her mind, of a happier time when Michael would cook her a hearty breakfasts. She dispelled it as quickly as it came. It would only make her cry again and she really didn't want to enter the meeting with swollen, red eyes, nor did she want to ruin this beautiful day. She put that memory back into the box inside her mind with all the other pain and locked it tightly.

Maggie sat in the car while she finished her meal. When she was done, she braced herself and walked into the Department of Highways office, where she met Ray Mills for her site briefing. Ray was an engineer on the Route 2 upgrade project. He explained to her that the National Historic Preservation Act and other federal laws require them to determine whether a proposed roadway project would significantly affect any archaeological sites or historic buildings. It would be her job to determine if anything of archaeological significance lay in the path of the newest stretch of the soon-to-be-built four-lane. She was given a few maps as well as plans showing the route surveyed, and then Ray offered to lead her to the starting point.

Maggie followed Ray seven miles south to a wide, graveled pull out on the east side of Route 2, where she had noticed surveying stakes the day before. The two got out of their vehicles and walked toward the stakes.

"This is where we will start in about a month, Dr. MacLeod. As you can see, this is going to be a real bear for us. We'll have to blast away most of that hillside ahead, because it's all rock. We did some improvements a few years ago for drainage and it took longer than we had expected. So, as you can imagine, we're anxious to get started on it."

Maggie looked around with a well-trained eye while she attempted to determine where she would start her investigation. "I'm sure I can be miles ahead a month from now," she said. "I'll keep you informed."

"Yeah, just call us immediately if there's a concern. I doubt if you'll find anything that will affect us, but you never know, and if you need anything let me know," Ray said, getting back in his pickup truck and heading back north on the highway.

"Thanks for that vote of confidence," Maggie muttered to herself, rolling her eyes. She looked at her watch to see it was only 8:45 AM. It would be forty-five minutes until her crew would arrive, so she looked over the space that would become the dig site to discern if there was anything close worth investigating. The sun was now burning the fog off the hills and the misty morning air was fresh and appealing. A small stream ran out of a hollow close by, grabbing her attention. She walked over to check it out. After looking the spot over, Maggie decided there was a chance that it might have been a choice place for at least an encampment at some time. She decided to set up shop 100 feet from the current highway. She opened the tailgate of the Suburban and spread out a few tools—a trowel, yellow tape, some brushes, a sieve, and a few plastic bags—just enough to get them through the day. Maggie then walked over to the stream and stepped about three feet down its muddy bank. The water was shallow enough to cross on top of the rocks, with some pools that formed in turns that looked much deeper. She turned over a rock and watched a crawdad swim away backwards, a pickup truck pulling up beside hers. Three people emerged—one man and two women—all college-aged and wearing jeans and t- shirts. Maggie dried her hands off on her shorts and walked to meet them.

"Hi, I'm Dr. Macleod. You must be my crew?" Maggie asked hopefully.

"I guess so," one of the girls said with a laugh, reaching to shake Maggie's hand. "I'm Ellen, and this is Rick, and Ally."

"Hi, guys. You can call me Maggie," Reaching out, she shook each of their hands. "So, are you all from around here?"

"I'm not. I'm from Katy, just outside of Houston, Texas," Ellen offered. Ellen was tall and very attractive. She had blonde hair with dark roots, and was wearing a lot of makeup. Something she would come to regret as the day wore on. She had a slight but unmistakable Texas accent and kept her hands folded across her lower abdomen like a debutante in a pageant.

"I'm from here," Rick replied, unfolding a pair of sunglasses and putting them on. Rick was skinny, of average height, with short dark hair.

"Oh good!" said Maggie. "Maybe you can keep us from getting lost, then."

"I'm from Morgantown," Ally chimed in, "but I have a friend in New Martinsville I am staying with for a few weeks. Rick and I are in the Native American Studies Program at WVU and next year I'll be going to grad school." Ally was a brunette, about 5'3", cute, with high cheekbones. She looked like she might be of Native American descent, as did Rick.

"Oh, that's wonderful," Maggie replied with a smile. "I expect we can learn a lot from each other in the coming weeks, then."

"I'm in the grad program," said Ellen. "Right now I have a degree in anthropology."

"So how does a gal from Texas pick West Virginia to go to college? Do they have a good program there?" asked Maggie, leading them toward her Suburban.

The three looked at each other and Ellen laughed, saying, "It's a party school! I mean, I am serious about my career, though."

"I should hope so." Maggie replied, looking back at them with a smile.

"This four-lane is going all the way down through the state, I guess," Rick interjected. "So we might have some other opportunities beyond right here, huh?"

"That's what I've heard," Maggie responded. "I'm not sure really, but I'll be elsewhere, I am sure of that." The four continued introductions for a time. Maggie guessed they were serious students and saw it as a chance to pass on some of her skills to them. Maybe even some of her knowledge. She felt good about that. She then handed each of them a folding trowel, leading them to the stream. "Look around and try to imagine what it was like here. Before roads, before you could see any buildings. Try to imagine how the inhabitants might have lived. We have the Ohio River nearby, and that would have been a source of transportation, maybe even some trade. There would have been plenty of food all around here, really. Areas along fields would have been choice for some sort of permanent lodging. So this might be a good place to start our investigating. Remember the inhabitants here would have lived in lodges, sometimes with a central fire ring. I'm sure they would have had areas for burial. Let's just have a quick look here and see if we find anything." The four of them went to work, slowly but ardently digging for signs that there had been life. There was some sporadic talk and laughter from the three students. Maggie, however, became fixed on one spot when she found some coal not far under the soil closer to the vehicles. It was curious to her that coal would be so close to the surface, so she decided to investigate thoroughly. The hours passed with a few breaks for water, with the students lost in conversation among themselves. Maggie got caught up in her own thoughts as well, once again dominated by Michael.

"Maggie! Hey, we're going to town for lunch. You want to go, or do you want me to pick you up something?" Rick asked.

Maggie wiped her brow, rose to her feet, and looked at the hillside behind her. "No, no thanks. I'm going to stretch my legs." She felt the awkward uncomfortable silence that fell upon the group and she realized that not accepting Rick's request was a bit rude. It was not often she felt like a fish out of water, but in this place it had become a common theme. She looked back over her shoulder to clarify, "I brought a banana. I want to take some pictures from up there before we get too far along on this." Maggie pointed to the top of the steep rock cliff that had loomed above them all day. Grabbing her backpack and camera, she started walking up the hillside, listening to the laughter of the others as they shut their car doors and pulled away.

The ground was carpeted with ferns, may apples, and briars, which she tried to work her way around. Maggie realized that her choice in shorts had been a bad idea. She would pay for that decision later. Less than 100 yards to the cliff and she was still unable to look beyond the forest canopy. Oaks, ash, and maples blocked her view. She took a fresh bottle of water from her pack, drinking it and examining the forest more closely. It was unlike any other she had seen before, its foliage thick and tall enough to blot out almost all of the light. Maggie thought that many species of birds must inhabit the area. She could hear a variety of different bird calls.

A sudden rustle of leaves near her feet startled her until she saw a chipmunk scurrying out of her path. It seemed to move magically, disappearing under ground cover, then reappearing on top of rocks and moss-covered limbs to look back at her. "So you're an Appalachian rat?" Maggie said with a smile as it scurried out of sight. Looking to her right, she could see the sandstone cliff and picked a route that would lead her easily to its top. She made her way closer to the rocks, the canopy giving way to a stunning view. She could now see the hills of Ohio, which ran down gently to a scant strand of cornfields along the Ohio River. The sandy banks were covered with driftwood bleached white from the sun. Finally, she approached the highest point on the cliff and slowly made her way to the edge.

Maggie looked below her boots to follow the rocks several hundred feet to the highway. Now she could see that the road sat on a shelf cut from the steep hillside a few hundred feet above the river. Soon the rock face, aged with time and partially covered with moss, would yield to blasts from explosives in preparation for the new four-lane. She wondered if her photos would be the last view of their beauty. A sudden feeling of vertigo made her take a step back from the edge. Taking a seat, she enjoyed the view that stretched out before her. Maggie removed the lens cap from her camera and started panning, taking pictures along the way. To the south she could see several miles down the river where a tugboat pulling barges of coal was disappearing around a bend. Its wake was the only interruption of the water, while further north the river was as smooth as glass.

Directly across the river from her were cornfields, and Maggie wondered how many centuries' inhabitants had been fed by crops grown along the fertile riverbanks. She sat on her perch high about the valley, imagining what peoples had occupied this place for thousands of years. The river, forest, and fields would have provided an abundance of food, shelter, and transportation. The area even might have been analogous to Mexico and South America, where civilizations thrived, but for some reason did not sustain growth. She realized that their disappearance must have been due to the western expansion of the 1700's and wondered where to look for clues. Surely there had to be some, somewhere.

As Maggie finished the last bites of her banana, she rose to her feet and saw a pickup truck pulling off the road. It parked beside her car and a person got out, slowly looking around, pacing even. She could tell that they were looking for someone and that someone was most likely her. Maggie headed down the hill at a quick pace to see who it was. She chose to ignore the many scratches from the briars cutting into her legs. She caught glimpses of the man looking over her site.

Maggie hurried as best she could but the descent was not an easy one. When she was less than 100 yards from him, the man looked at her, tipped his ball cap, and smiled, stepping away from the open tailgate of her Suburban. Maggie slowed her pace, catching her breath and approaching the man. He was tall, about 6' 2", with broad shoulders under a denim shirt stretched tightly across his muscled chest. He wore to tight jeans that accentuated... everything. His dark complexion and high cheekbones were strongly suggestive of Native American descent. He was clean-shaven and had a friendly smile with an intimidating stance—a veritable abundance of contradictions that heightened Maggie's senses. If she didn't know herself better, she could have sworn she felt rush of heat, the telltale sign of a blush coming on. "Can I help you?" Maggie asked flustered, passing him and looking over her gear.

"You've got to be Dr. Macleod," he said, offering his hand. "I'm Ben Adams."

Maggie did not face him, but briefly looked around. A shovel had been moved from where she had been digging and she grabbed it quickly, tossing it back to its previous spot. Irritated, she turned to face him, folding her arms. "Oh, Ben is it then? Well, Ben, are you in the habit of crossing yellow tape? Not a wise habit."

"No, ma'am, I'm sorry. I guess I'm just so used to pulling off the road here when I don't think I can wait until I get home to piss." Looking shocked, Maggie viewed the ground around her as if expecting to see dampness. Ben squatted down and started examining a sieve, with a laugh "I'm just kidding. I'm sorry if..."

"Please, don't touch anything here!" Maggie said abruptly, grabbing the sieve from his hands. "I'm at a very sensitive section of the excavation here."

She knew that Ben must have taken stock of the scene, realizing that she had all but just begun her search. She saw him fight the urge to smile. "Well the only thing you're likely to find here are some .22 casings, and maybe a beer can. Anyway, I'm Ben Adams and I'm from the ANAWV, and..."

Maggie shook her head, looking Ben in the eyes. "The what?"

"The Appalachian Native Americans...of West Virginia. Well, actually my grandfather and some of the elders in the ANA asked me to observe, and to make sure...hey, is that Etta James?" Ben asked, poking his head into Maggie's car, grabbing a CD and drawing a quick response.

"Yes! Yes, that's Etta James. Look, I am in charge here," she said, looking him over, "so you are the one. The ANN you say?"

"ANA."

"Well, my question to you, Mr. Adams, is what gives you the authority to be poking around my site?" Maggie stood resolute with her feet apart and arms crossed like the bouncer of an exclusive nightclub. Ben took a few seconds, as if to choose his words in an attempt to defuse an already tense situation. He removed his ball cap, revealing a sleek mane of long black hair, and wiped his brow. "Well, the truth is, I have no authority at all, but the artifacts you're digging up belong to my ancestors and the tribe. We just want to make sure any burial grounds and other things sacred to my people are treated with respect, that's all."

"I see," Maggie said, looking inside her vehicle again, making sure everything was there. "Well, you can see we've only just begun our work here. You are more than welcome to observe today, as long as you don't touch anything."

"I'll try not to ruin any of the bottle caps," Ben answered sarcastically.

Maggie picked up two rusty bottle caps from the tailgate of the Suburban and threw them in a trashcan that was tied to a mile maker post on the pull out. She then grabbed a sieve, and stepped over the yellow tape and down into a trench; it had been dug four feet wide and was barely a foot deep. Ben followed her seconds later.

"Please watch where you step," Maggie said condescendingly. She knew she was being very hard, a bitch even, but she didn't know how to stop. Her emotional thermostat seemed to be stuck at Super B today and she wasn't sure why. Maybe it was the heat, the humidity, or both. It was then that Bev's words echoed in her head..."Show him every kindness, Mags! Do not embarrass me or the museum!"

"Damn," she cursed under her breath. Maggie didn't care for her attitude either.

She looked up and noticed that Ben had put his hands in his pants pockets, a mischievous smile on his face. He watched her examine some soil with a small vein of coal running through it. "Can you typically find coal so close to the surface in this area?" she asked, trying to be a bit softer in her approach.

Ben looked at where she had been digging and said, "Yep. Especially near highways and railroad tracks. It's probably just where some coal truck lost some."

Maggie continued, not wanting to argue as they heard a vehicle pull off the road behind them.

Chapter 5

"Sahale!" Rick yelled, shutting the door of his truck. Ben walked toward them with no regard to where his feet landed. "Hey, Rick! Good to see you. My god, it's the middle of the day and you're picking up women already."

"Hey!" Ally hollered, skipping to Ben and giving him a hug. "What brings you here?"

"I'm just here to observe, make sure you don't pocket any arrowheads or anything."

"This is our friend Ellen, and it looks like you already met Maggie," Ally said.

"Hello, Ellen, I'm Ben Adams. You can call me Ben, or Sahale," he said with a laugh, looking at Rick and winking.

Ellen adjusted her shirt and jeans, walking up to Ben and offering her hand. "Hi, Ben," she said with a flirtatious voice. "Do you live around here?"

"Yeah, not far. I teach at the college. I know Rick and Ally from being over at Morgantown a few times. Dr. MacLeod was just showing me around. Are you guys going to look at other places?"

"Yes," Maggie said suddenly, approaching them from behind. "Maybe up on the hill where they are going to blast." She got her camera out of the Suburban and walked to where she was digging to take a few pictures.

"Glad I'm dressed for it, then," Ben said through clinched teeth, looking at Rick with a smile.

"We're going out tonight if you'd like to join us," Ellen said to Ben.

"You know, I just might do that," he answered.

Maggie watched and listened to the four of them, and was almost to the point of asking them to return to work when the group broke up. Ellen and Ally went off on their own, while Ben walked with Rick to the base of the hill across the stream. Later, while Maggie was taking a water break, she noticed she could only see the three students. Her strange observer was nowhere in sight. "Rick, did Ben leave?" she asked, trying not to sound overly concerned.

"He took off up the hill there, Maggie," Rick replied, pointing to approximately the same path that Maggie had taken earlier. Maggie looked through the thick trees for a time, but seeing nothing, continued what she was doing. Nearly two hours later Maggie heard the brush crack up the hillside and saw Ben coming off the hill, covered with sweat and wearing a leather bag across his shoulder. He walked over to Rick and started talking when Ellen cried out from across the field on the other side of some thick briars.

"Maggie! I found something!" Maggie worked her way around the briars to Ellen, who stood smiling, showing off an arrowhead. It was almost three inches long and of obvious shape. As Maggie approached, she raced to beat Ben there and examined the piece.

"Well, this is a start," Maggie scrutinized the piece of flint. She rubbed more of the dirt off it and then looked around the area where Ellen had found it.

"Would you believe that's my first arrowhead?" Ellen said, looking directly at Ben.

"You might find several around in this area," Ben replied. "Nice work." He smiled at Ellen and patted her shoulder. Maggie continued to look over the immediate area as the others talked. After more searching, nothing else turned up. Maggie looked at her watch and said, "Okay, guys, let's call it a day. Let's meet here at seven in the morning and we'll start working our way up the hill. It's supposed to be hot tomorrow, so I thought we would begin earlier. Sound good?" The others agreed.

"Hey, Maggie, we're going out tonight. Care to join us?" Ally asked.

"No, I'm afraid that I have some work I need to do and I don't want to be out late."

"You're going to have to eat tonight aren't you? Why don't we all get together about 8 for dinner, my treat?" Ben asked, looking at Maggie.

Maggie eyed Ben, his ball cap soiled and ringed with sweat. She really wanted to be alone but thought it would be the sociable thing to do to join them. "All right, I suppose I could do that. Thank you, Ben. Eight o'clock then?"

"Where are we going?" asked Rick.

"I thought maybe Sally's. I haven't had a steak in a long time," said Ben. "Does that sound good?"

"That sounds fine," Maggie answered, envisioning a steakhouse.

"You want me to pick you up?" Ben asked.

"No, I'm not staying out late, as I said. I will meet you there."

"Okay," said Ben. "It's easy to find. It's just right along Route 2 here on your right, just as you get into New Martinsville. You'll see a marquee out front."

"I'll find it, thanks," Maggie replied. She could not remember seeing a restaurant there, but hoped it would be in plain sight.

"All right then," Rick agreed as the others got into their vehicles, "we'll be there!"

They all drove away and Maggie returned to the Dogwood Inn. She carried her other two bags of luggage inside with her and was greeted by Troy when she walked in the door.

"Miss MacLeod, I have your packages right here," Troy said, pointing to two boxes beside the front desk.

"Oh, thank you, Troy. Could you have them carried over to my Suburban across the street? I'll be right back down as soon as I put these bags in my room."

"I sure can," he said, picking up a box with a grunt. Maggie watched him as she walked up the steps to her room. She put the two bags on the floor and raced down to help, but she could see Troy carrying the second box across the street. He sounded winded and she opened the tailgate of the vehicle for him.

"You didn't have to get them both. Those are rather heavy."

"Oh, that's all right," Troy replied, placing the box on the tailgate. "That's what I'm here for. You need help with anything else?"

"No, I'm all moved over now," she said. "I'm meeting my crew at a place called Sally's later. Have you eaten there?"

"Oh yes. It's good food. It's just on this side of New Martinsville, right along the highway."

"Okay, thanks." She turned and the two walked back to the Inn. Maggie went to her room, opened the door, and immediately the picture of Michael and her brothers caught her eye like it was illuminated with spotlights. She had a good first day; she managed to keep her mind on her work for the most part, but now felt so lonely and secluded from the world, shutting the door behind her. For the first time since getting there she turned on the TV and started hunting for a news channel, removing her hiking boots. Finally she found CNN and sat on the sofa. Several more troops were killed by a car bomb in Iraq, the body of a girl who had been missing for weeks had been found near Atlanta, and outside her room there was not a sound. It was like she was isolated in a bunker deep in the Appalachians. After resting some, Maggie decided to have a hot bath. She took off her clothes and sat on the edge of her bed, touching the picture on the night stand as the tub filled with hot water. Once full, she added some bubble bath that she had brought with her and sank into the tub. The hot water soothed her muscles, tired from the trek up the mountain, and she massaged the dried blood from the cut on her legs left by the briars. This was exactly what her mood needed.

Chapter 6

*M*aggie started to get dressed for dinner and realized she had a dilemma. Knowing nothing about the place they were to meet left her with no idea of what to wear. Taking no chances, she picked out a long, full, bohemian skirt with a blue flowered design, and a short-sleeved white cotton blouse. After putting her hair up, she picked out some sandals to complete her outfit. Looking herself over in the full-length mirror, she was satisfied with her look. Leaving a light on, she headed downstairs. It was 7:30 PM and Troy was still sitting behind the desk, reading a book. "Have a nice evening, Miss MacLeod," he said.

Maggie returned the smile, nodding when she passed.

Twenty minutes later she approached New Martinsville and looked around for the restaurant. Ahead on the right side of the road was a marquee, rusted and resting on three legs and with some letters missing. It read, "THUR L VE BAND RIDGE RUN ERS 9-1." The parking lot was mostly full, but the building looked more like a barn to her. It had weathered wood siding, gravel sidewalk, and a steel drum half full of beer bottles close to the door. She wondered whether to keep driving, but then saw Rick's truck parked in the lot. Maggie picked out a place to park where she felt the rented Suburban would be safe. "Wow...am I in the right place?" She said to herself, watching people come and go. They looked like construction workers with muddy clothes and hard hats. Before checking her face in the mirror, she wondered if it was a good idea or not to actually get out of the truck at all. While doing so, she saw Ben's truck pull in behind her. Pretending not to notice, she got out and shut the door without looking back.

"Maggie," Ben called out to her, "I see you found us all right."

"Oh, hi, Ben. Yes," Maggie said, studying the outside of the building, "I sure did."

She turned to greet him and noticed that he still looked just as good to her as he had earlier. Taking note that he had cleaned up, she marveled at his choice of the loud tropical shirt he wore. It unnerved her a bit with all its pinks, greens, and yellows. The colors were so bright that she was sure they would glow under a black light. The thought of that brought a smile to her red lips. It was sure a conversation starter! She fought the urge to laugh out loud from the mental picture of him standing in a dark room, shirt ablaze in color. It was then that Maggie noticed the top few buttons were undone, giving her a faint hint of the bronzed, muscled chest that lay beneath all those silly colors. She felt her lips go dry and she looked away suddenly, feeling like her body had betrayed her. There was no way it should be reacting this way to him. "Damn it." The curse slipped from her lips and she felt a stab of regret.

Ben caught up with her. "What did you say?" he questioned, pulling the door open for her. "By the way, you clean up nice, Maggie!"

The sound of AC/DC hit her ears as they walked inside. Before she could reply to his compliment, she noticed how very busy the place was. The bar was full of people ordering drinks. Looking to her left, she was happy to see a regulation pool table, and there was a group of people shooting what looked to be like a very intense game. Ellen was among them. To her right was an adjacent dining room with a stage at one end. She wondered if there might be live music later. Nearly every table was full and waitresses in shorts and t-shirts whisked by them, singing along with Bon Scott.

As they looked across the room they caught sight of two sets of waving hands where Rick and Ally had saved them a large, round, corner booth.

Another man standing beside Rick yelled above the noise,

"Sahale!"

"Hey!" yelled Ben, slapping the other man on the back.

"Maggie, I love your skirt!" Ally hollered to her above all the noise. She stood up to greet them and Maggie was in awe of her choice: a tight pink t-shirt with the Playboy bunny on it. That was a bold choice for a girl of her age. Maggie had to wonder if Ally had aspirations of being a bunny herself. "Thanks, Ally. I really didn't know what..."

Just then Ellen came bumping into their shoulders, interrupting with, "I beat his ass!" then high-fiving Ally.

Maggie smiled at her warmly. "Way to go, Ellen," she said, taking note of the very low- cut top Ellen had on. Quite a difference than her attire from this afternoon. However, Maggie had looked quite different, too.

"Who did you beat?" asked Ben.

"That guy over there in the flannel shirt with the sleeves cut out, searching in his pockets for his balls!" Ellen said, laughing and pointing.

"Well, you ain't played me yet, Miss Houston," Ben responded, sitting down and scooting to the center of the booth. Ellen followed close behind when Ben motioned for everyone to join them. He reached for the menus, passing them out to everyone.

"The steaks are very good, Maggie. So are the burgers," Ally said, looking at her menu.

"Looks like a red meat eater's paradise, all right," Maggie joked.

"Aye, but you won't be findin' Haggis on there," Ben said in his best Scottish accent, referring to the traditional Scottish dish.

"Get a burger then, ya wee girl! Head, pants, now!" Rick answered back as they all laughed. "Man, I love 'So I Married an Axe Murderer'! Mike Meyers is amazing!" he added.

Maggie was unfamiliar with the movie reference, but still smiled politely and continued looking at the menu as a waitress came over to take their order.

"What can I get you all tonight?... Hey there, Ben!" she said, bending over the table to write.

"Hi," said Ben. "Bring us a pitcher of whatever these three are drinking." As the waitress left Maggie noticed Rick whispering something to Ben, who then laughed. Maggie and Ally continued looking over the menu and Ellen sat with an icy mug to her lips.

The waitress returned shortly with mugs and a pitcher of beer before taking their orders. Ben reached out for the pitcher and filled the mugs. After the waitress rushed off with their orders, Ben raised his glass and said, "A toast...to our ancestors. May we always respect them." It was somber enough to elicit silence from the group for a moment, then Ben asked, "So, Maggie, where do you call home?"

"Boston, actually," Maggie started after a sip from the mug, "but I haven't spent much time there the past few years. I've been in Mexico, all over South America, the Middle East."

"Oh my, now see? That's what I want to do," Ellen joined the conversation. "I want to travel a lot as soon as I get out of graduate school. My heart will always be in Texas, but there's less humid places."

Maggie laughed, replying, "And more humid ones."

"I would love South America," Ally responded, "I think. I can't imagine working somewhere like that, with beautiful scenery, and away from the hassles of the industrial world."

"It's nice. I'll show you some photos I took, but you have to remember, it's not like you can run to Super Wal-Mart in the middle of the night for bug spray, or Tylenol. You can't even make phone calls until certain hours, even in the best of locations."

"Kmart, then?" Ben joked.

"What's the coolest thing you've unearthed, Maggie?" Rick asked.

"I would have to say...in Peru, five years ago, I was working with...a friend, and we found a small room in an Inca village that had not been pillaged by the Spanish. The bodies still had some gold jewelry on them. That was exciting."

"Oh my god!" exclaimed Ellen. "I would be struttin' out of the jungle wearing it."

Maggie managed to tell two more stories involving Michael without mentioning his name. Ellen flirted with Ben, and he and Rick seemed to be surveying the room as more people filed in. The group continued talking until their food arrived, then Maggie asked, "Fries, on top of my steak salad?"

"Mm, that looks good, Maggie. Wish I would have ordered one," Ben said, cutting into his rare porterhouse.

"I think I just heard Ben's steak moo!" Rick laughed.

"Hey, I wanna taste the meat."

When another pitcher of beer arrived, Maggie and Ally asked for water. The conversations, however, maintained a nice balance, allowing everyone to get to know one another better. Everyone declined desert and an uncomfortable silence overtook the table, until Ally commented, "Maggie, you have such beautiful hair."

"Oh, thank you," Maggie said, blushing and gently fingering her curls with her fingertips. She looks cute when she blushes, Ben thought. He had noticed that she played with her curls when she was embarrassed or nervous. It was strangely endearing. She had taken his breath away, when he first saw her sprinting out of the woods with her cheeks flushed and her eyes aflame with outrage at his perusing through her things. She had looked breathtaking then, he thought, until he had seen her tonight. She had tried to wrestle her wild curls into a twist on top of her head, but the unruly mass did not stay contained and stray curls had escaped to frame her round face. Ben spotted the two beautiful jeweled combs sticking out of the sea of red. Both held sapphires, matching the blue of her skirt. They glittered in Maggie's luminous auburn locks, complimenting it and giving her an almost regal glow.

Ben was captivated; even in the dimly lit booth she managed to be graceful and painfully beautiful. Lost in his thoughts, he hadn't noticed Maggie had turned to look at him. His eyes wandered to her face and they locked gazes. Ben panicked for a second when he realized that he had been staring at her like a moonstruck teenager, but managed to pull himself together. He hoped she wouldn't notice how much her beauty had rattled him. His pants had grown tight, and he shifted uncomfortably, smiling at her with a confidence he didn't feel.

"The combs are beautiful. Those are real sapphires, aren't they?" Ben asked, trying to deflect from his blatant stare.

"Yes, they are," Maggie replied. "Lucky guess, or do you know jewels?"

"Fake ones are a darker, more saturated blue. You can spot them easily, actually. Yours are...quite beautiful."

"Oh my god, Maggie! Did you get them on one of your trips?" Ellen chimed in, leaning over to brush some curls out of the way to get a better look. Damn, I wish I could run my fingers through her hair. I wonder how it would feel to twist my fist into it as I ... Ben felt his heart speed up, his hands beginning to sweat, and his breath caught in his throat. His reaction to her surprised him. Could she be...?

"Yes, in Peru. They were given to me as...as a gift," Maggie said, in an attempt to avoid a memory of Michael. The two were in a tourist village in Peru, leisurely strolling past shops. When Maggie felt a tug on her arm, she turned. Michael was staring into one of the display windows, his eyes alight like a child at a toy store. Maggie followed his gaze, but nothing specifically special caught her attention. The display window held some baubles and random pieces of jewel. She looked up at Michal questioningly and he gently grabbed her chin, slowly turning it towards a set of combs. She remembered his exact words: "Those combs, the gold ones with the sapphires. Maggie, I don't care what they cost, they were made for you!" He had let go of her and headed into the store. Maggie had smiled at his eagerness and graciously accepted his gift when he returned to her side. She had worn them ever since, and they had become part of her most precious belongings.

Ellen broke Maggie's train of thought by nudging her and laughing. "You didn't sneak them out of that Inca site, did you, Maggie?"

Maggie shook her head. She laughed nervously, holding the back of her neck.

Ben noticed the faraway look in her eyes after her response to Ellen. He wondered what had gone through her mind. By her nervous laugh and body language he knew that whatever it was it was painful. He wanted to ask her, but was afraid that it was neither the right time nor place for that. He had to stop his sudden urge to take her in his arms. She would likely get angry at the sudden familiarity, so he decided to just take another swig of his beer and observe her out of the corner of his eye.

She really is exquisite. Her complexion was flawless and smooth. Ben imagined that it must be incredibly soft to the touch. His fingertips tingled, yearning to touch her. Completely oblivious to his scrutiny, she threw her head back and giggled. He couldn't help but follow her graceful neck, to her slender shoulders, her fragile collarbone and down to a glimpse of an ample cleavage. He heard her clear her throat, which snapped him out of his musings. Looking up, he locked gazes with her and grinned. Ben shrugged.

"Well, someone knows how to buy gifts, I guess. They are perfect for you, Maggie."

Dinner had been fun and Maggie noted that Ben was quite the gentleman for picking up the bill for them all. It was late though and Maggie was ready to go home.

"I have to get going," Maggie told them. "I have a few things left to do before I turn in tonight."

"Whoa, whoa, hold on! Y'all don't have to rush off so fast," Ben said quickly.

"It's 9:30, Ben," Ally replied, looking at her watch.

"My friend's band is about to go on, guys. Come on. Stay for a few songs. They are worth it, I promise."

"All right, I'll stay just a while longer," Ally said, returning to her seat. Maggie sighed. She was tired and ready to go to bed, but Ben's pleading eyes made her reconsider. She sat back down.

The band started playing Lynard Skynard and the raucous, mostly redneck crowd wailed its approval. Maggie liked them. Ben had been right. The band was worth sticking around for. Two songs later, the band changed gears from their fast paced tunes to something a bit more sedate. Rick grabbed Ally by the hand, inviting her to dance, and the two headed to the dance floor. Ellen left for another game of pool, leaving Maggie alone at the table with Ben. They sat in silence for a moment.

Finally, Ben looked at Maggie and asked, "Would you like to dance?" She was hesitant, really wanting to head home, but didn't want to offend Ben, so she agreed.

The floor was packed with people, making it hard not to bump into other couples. Occasionally someone would say hi to Ben. Finally, Maggie asked, "Do you know everyone in here?"

"It's not a huge community." Ben laughed and continued, "I guess I do know most of them."

"It's a little different, from home, I mean," Maggie said, looking around the room.

"Yeah, I like it here."

"Well...I didn't mean better, I just meant different."

"Oh, I know," said Ben, trying to avoid an argument.

"Well, I'm glad I have a good crew here. Everyone has made

me feel right at home and I'm looking forward to working with Ally, Rick, and Ellen. They seem like good people."

"So...what time did you say tomorrow?"

"Oh, will you be joining us again tomorrow?" Maggie asked bluntly.

"Yes, like I said, I've been asked to represent the people, and I thought I might be of some help."

"Well, we do have a lot of work to do..."

"No worries. I will stay out of your way," he promised with a smile.

Maggie didn't want to be rude but she really needed him to understand that she was in charge of this project.

Ben really enjoyed the feel of his hands on the small of Maggie's back. He had been a little nervous to ask her to dance, even expected her to decline, but was happy that he had managed to get his courage up. In general he didn't ask ladies to dance, since he had two left feet at times and didn't really care to make an ass of himself; but he really wanted to be close to Maggie.

The scent of her perfume rose gently from her neck, even above the cigarette smoke of the bar. Ben looked down at her face, her eyes sparkling in the dim light, and his eyes settled on her lush, perfectly red lips. As if she was subconsciously feeling his gaze on her, Maggie bit on her bottom lip sending a little chill down his spine.

Ben had planned to make small talk, yet he couldn't think of anything to say and before he knew it the song came to an end. Maggie politely thanked him as he walked her back to their seats. As soon as they arrived, Maggie leaned over to grab her purse.

"Thanks again for dinner, Ben. I really have to get going."

"Aww, okay, Maggie. I'm glad you came," Ben said, placing his hand on her shoulder.

"Goodnight, Ben."

"See ya tomorrow," he replied and watched as Maggie turned to say her goodbyes to the others. He had a hard time tearing his gaze from her. He watched her graceful form weave her way through the crowd, only to disappear out the door. A gentle tap on his shoulder broke his gaze. He turned to see who it was. "Kim!" he yelled, hugging her. "I haven't seen you since... Fourth of July, wasn't it?"

Chapter 7

The ride back to the Inn seemed short. Maybe it was just Maggie acclimating to the area. She could not say for sure. Hard as she tried, she could not find anything wrong with this place. Sistersville, New Martinsville—they held a certain charm and friendliness of small towns that was lacking in Boston, for sure. Maggie smiled, pulling the Suburban into the lot across from the Inn. Not quite ten pm and the streets were almost rolled up. She got out of the truck and took a deep breath. The cool night air was filled with the scent of flowering Dogwoods. They dotted the landscape almost everywhere, their pink blossoms unmistakable among the hills of green.

She leaned against the truck, not wanting to give up the view of the star-lit sky. One could see all of the constellations here, without the bright lights of the big city to interfere. Why am I beginning to feel so at home here?' Maggie wondered. This place seemed to have a strange effect on her. Today had been the first day in she didn't know how long that she did not cry. She had actually laughed a few times, much to her surprise. Michael had been in her thoughts...he always was, but the work had kept her busy today. There had not been time for tears. Maggie wasn't sure she liked that.

"I will never forget," she whispered into the cool night air. Taking a deep breath, she shoved off the truck and made her way across the street to the Inn. Walking through the doors, she noticed that Troy was sitting at the front desk reading the paper. The light in the lobby was so dim and she wondered how he could possibly see the print without hopelessly straining his eyesight. Troy looked up and met her with a warm smile.

"How was your evening, Ms. MacLeod?"

Maggie returned the smile and answered, "It was nice, thank you. Good food, good conversation, and a beautiful night. What more could I ask for?"

"Glad you had a good evening."

"Me too. It has been a while since I laughed," she said, looking down at the floor. It seemed such a simple phrase, but she somehow felt mixed up. Looking up, she replied, "I have to be at the site at seven in the morning. Is there any chance that I can pick up breakfast for six people? I'd like to have my crew start the day off right."

Troy smiled. "Of course. I will see to it myself." "Thank you," Maggie said. "You just rest well tonight, Ms. MacLeod." "Maggie, please call me Maggie," she

insisted. "Well, goodnight, Maggie." "Good night, Troy, and thank you for being so helpful," she said before she turned and headed up the stairs to her room.

* * *

Strong, calloused hands moved over her bare back and Maggie closed her eyes, relishing the touch. "My God, I am a lucky man." His breath was soft on her skin.

Maggie giggled, "Yes, you are and don't you forget it, mister!" Her words were playful. "I just love the way the light plays on your skin. Your hair. You are so beautiful, Maggie."

She felt his fingers softly tangle in her auburn locks. Opening her eyes, she watched the candlelight cast shadows across the whole room. "Flattery will get you everywhere," she snickered. The fire in the fireplace was at full roar and it added to the shadow play. Maggie had not been sure what to expect when he had asked her over for dinner. She didn't even know he cooked. His apartment had been a pleasant surprise. Expecting a typical bachelor pad, she was amazed at how homey it truly was, and now, as she lay naked, sprawled across the large, antique bed, she realized that she never wanted to leave this place. This evening had been perfect, and she wanted it to last forever.

"Will it now?" he questioned with a smile.

Lord, he's beautiful. The thought came to her when she took in the sight of him. His blond hair was almost covering his face when he leaned down to look at her naked body. His body was tan from hours of work in the sun and brawny from hours spent in the gym. That was a passion she herself did not share, but it sure looked good on him. He looked up and met her gaze. His eyes were so blue; she marveled at their ability to change colors. They could go from the bright blue of the sky to the dark grey- blue of the ocean in seconds, depending on his mood. All she could see now was wide open blue sky in them.

His hands made their way down her back and over the silky smooth skin of her naked bottom. Squeezing a cheek gently, his other hand moved lower and parted her legs slightly. His fingers made long, slow strokes against her velvet softness until he found his mark. Maggie felt a stirring deep inside her.

"Michael!" she gasped.

* * *

Maggie sat up with a start, gasping for breath. She reached up and pushed her lush curls off her face. Beads of sweat had begun to form on her forehead and down her chest. Her satin chemise was wet and clung to her chest almost unbearably tight.

"Damn it!" she cried, feeling her tears stinging in her eyes. Feeling the breath rush out of her, she fought off the painful sobs that dared to steal her breath forever. Switching on the lamp next to her bedside table, she took in her surroundings. Everything was just as she left it, her clothes still strewn across the floor. She had really fallen in love with this room, with the Inn itself, but now that charm offered her no comfort. Just silence. Maggie looked at the bedside table, reaching for the photograph. How could I betray you by looking at another man? She clutched it tightly, until her knuckles turned white.

"Oh, Michael!" she cried.

She laid down, pulling her legs up close. Her sobs filled the room, stealing her breath with them. She cried, got angry, and cried again until sleep took her once more. This time, she did not dream.

Chapter 8

Six had come too early. Maggie had hit the snooze button of her whining alarm clock at least five times. Eventually, she managed to pull herself out of bed and get ready for the long day that lay ahead. After her brush with the briers yesterday, she had opted for khaki pants and a white t-shirt. She pulled her way-too-curly hair back, securing it with a baseball cap. The humidity and her hair seemed to be at war. Her auburn curls had always been somewhat of a trademark, but in humidity they surpassed tiny ringlets and she always ended up looking like a poodle.

Maggie put her laptop in her bag, swung it over her shoulder, and reached for her sunglasses before heading downstairs. Troy looked up from his desk and gave her a warm smile. He raised a finger and pushed his glasses up his nose. She could not help but smile back at him.

"Breakfast is almost packed up, Maggie. I packed two carafes of coffee too. I assumed you'd want that as well as orange juice."

Maggie descended the last of the steps and crossed the multi-colored carpeted floor to the desk. To her surprise, Ben sat in a chair next to it. The banister had obscured her view of him.

"Thank you, Troy," she said softly.

Ben stood up. "Good Morning, Maggie. I hope you don't mind, but I thought we could ride out to the site together this morning. I have some information about the area I would like to share with you."

"I would like that," she said, greeting him with a smile.

Ben looked pretty much the same as he had before. His dark hair was pulled back and held at the nape of his neck. He wore a tan work shirt with a very tight white t-shirt under it, accentuating his broad, sturdy shoulders. A pair of jeans and hiking boots finished his look. His sunglasses were pushed up on top of his head. Maggie found herself staring and she looked away quickly.

"Let me go check and see if everything is ready for you," Troy said.

They both watched him make his way down the hall and back to the kitchen. Ben met her glance again and smiled warmly. "You look nice this morning."

Maggie looked down at her appearance with a sigh, "About as good as a digger can look."

"Well, I like it. You're ready for anything in that outfit and you don't have any fancy shoes to worry about. You're my kind of girl, Ahawi."

She felt her brow wrinkle as she looked at him. "Ahawi?" she questioned.

"Think of it as your Native nickname…"

Troy came back, interrupting their conversation. He held a big box in one arm and two bags in the other. "All ready," he said.

Ben reached to take the box from him, while Maggie took the two bags.

"What do I owe you?" she questioned.

"Sahale took care of it already," Troy replied.

Maggie looked at Ben with surprise and said,

"That's not necessary." "My treat. It's the least I can do for getting on your nerves yesterday."

"Oh, well I…you didn't…"

Ben laughed softly. "It's okay, Ahawi. To know me is to love me," he said with a wink.

Maggie smirked. "Well, we best get going. I don't want the kids waiting around for us. Thank you, Troy."

"Not a problem, Maggie. Have a good day," he said, watching the two make their way outside and across the street.

The sun greeted the morning sky with orange streaks. Maggie thought how pretty it was while opening the back of the Suburban for Ben. He set the box down and she placed the bags next to it. Getting into the car, they were on the road in a matter of minutes.

"How are you liking it here?" Ben's voice broke the silence between them.

"I am adjusting well. It's very pretty here. Take the sky for instance, we don't get these colors in Boston much."

"It is beautiful country, but not much around. Most shopping and such is two hours in either direction. It could be hard for someone from the city to adjust."

Maggie smiled at the accusation and replied, "I am used to bringing everything I need with me. Shopping has never been high on my list."

"Ah, that's right. I remember you saying something like that last night. Like I said, my kind of girl." A silence formed between them. Maggie felt a little uncomfortable, taking in the scenery flying by. "Troy says he heard you crying last night," Ben said casually.

Maggie pressed her foot to the brake pedal and stopped in the middle of the two-lane road. Ben turned toward her, surprised.

"What did you say?" she questioned.

"Troy said you were crying last night. He was worried, thought I should check on you this morning, and if we are going to talk here, you'd best pull off the road. I have pull with the state cops, but I'm not sure I could save you from a ticket."

She pulled the truck over to the shoulder and put it in park. "He heard me?" Her hands met her face, feeling defeated.

"Well, you are the only guest at the Inn right now. It's an old building. Voices tend to carry. He was just concerned. I don't want to pry, just thought I should check on you is all."

Maggie felt herself fall forward to the steering wheel. Her face felt hot. She was embarrassed and crying now was making it worse.

"Hey," he said softly. His hand gently touched her shoulder.

She felt a sob come to her and she tried to stifle it, but it was no use. The floodgates had opened.

"It's okay, Ahawi. It's better to let it out than to keep it in.

Can I help?" he questioned with true concern.

Maggie didn't know where to begin. How could she tell her troubles to a man she just met? She pulled back from the steering wheel and met his glance. There was a look of true concern in his eyes. She did not know why, but she felt she could tell him anything and not have to worry about him smothering her like her family did. Ben reached up and met a tear that had escaped her long lashes.

"Your spirit is in turmoil," he whispered. "It's one of the first things I noticed about you."

She reached up and wiped the tears off her face. "I, um...I shouldn't be doing this. We hardly know each other and you're just trying to be nice. I shouldn't take advantage of you like this."

"Ahh, so you will bury yourself in your work like you always do? How's that been working out for you?" Ben questioned with a smirk on his face.

A flash of anger came to her, turning her red face a darker shade of scarlet. "What the hell do ya' know about me and my work? Everything is fine! I am fine!" All control on her accent had been lost.

"Oh yeah, sure you are. That's why we're sitting here on the shoulder of the road with you in tears!" he snapped back.

"How dare ya' judge me! You wouldn't even be here if you hadn't lied to me! Telling me you had information on the area? That's nice!"

"I didn't lie to you Maggie! Ray called me last night to tell me that they are going to be blasting up on the hill today. He wanted you to be aware so that you could keep your crew out of the way. You are supposed to stop by the road office and pick up hard hats for everyone."

Maggie looked puzzled. "Why didn't he call me?"

"Because you have a shitty attitude and frankly he doesn't want to deal with you!" As soon as he said it, he knew it had been a mistake. Bringing his hands to his mouth, he looked out the window.

She got out of the truck and paced back and forth. Suddenly she kicked the front tire and let out a scream at the top of her lungs. Ben got out, applauding her efforts.

"Now that's more like it! Get mad! Let it out!" he shouted

right along with her.

Maggie kicked the tire again. "I have never had a problem with people likin' me!" she said, throwing her hands up in the air in exasperation. Bringing her hands to her face again, she leaned back against the wheel well. Listening, she heard Ben walk around the front of the truck and felt his presence next to her.

"You might try being nicer to folks, then," he said softly.

"I was...I..." was all she could get out.

"You've been a little short with everyone, Maggie. Take me for instance. You assumed that I was just some annoyance yesterday. Someone who couldn't possibly know what they were doing. Someone who was going to cause you grief, and then, I had to beg you to come out with us last night. You were so sure you wouldn't enjoy our company..."

"No, that's na' it. That's not why I did na' want to go out," she began in protest. Meeting his warm brown eyes, she fought the urge to slap him. "I have been burying myself in my work and distancing myself from everyone and anyone."

"And why would you do that? What are you running from, Ahawi?" Ben placed his arm around her shoulders, trying to comfort her.

Maggie closed her eyes. Ma had been right. Things were beginning to creep up on her. She didnot know how much longer she could hold them at bay. *What was I thinkin' coming all the way out here?* she wondered. She took a deep breath and let it out slowly before she spoke. "Six months ago, I was on a dig in Mexico. Things went badly."

"Badly? How?"

"I lost someone. One of our pits caved in and we did na' get him out in time."

"Someone...someone that was close to you. Am I right?" Ben asked with caution.

"Michael..." Her voice cracked and she swallowed hard. "Michael, my fiancé. It was two weeks before our wedding," she said, trying to keep the emotion out of her voice.

Ben let out a soft whistle, the kind of sound that people make when they are astounded by what they have just heard. He tried to take cues from her body, wondering if it would be okay to pull her close. He realized then that she was already in his arms, hers wrapped around him tightly.

"What are you doing here?" he questioned.

"I need to work. It keeps me grounded, but at night..."

"That's when it's bad." Ben pat her back gently.

Maggie nodded her head in agreement to his statement. Taking a deep breath, he pulled her closer. His grandfather had been right, the deer with the broken heart came into his life and now all he wanted to do was to take her pain away. Instead, all he had accomplished was being an insensitive jerk. He took in the sweet smell of her hair, enjoyed the feeling of her body pressed to his. Her spirit was broken and he would do his best to try and mend it.

Maggie pulled away and broke the spell. "I'm sorry. I didn't mean to lay this on you. I'm usually better about keeping things to myself. You just seem..."

"Easy to talk to?" he questioned with a smile.

Maggie felt a smile come to her too, relaxing a bit. How long had it been since she had done that? "Yes. Very easy. It's too bad you're such a jerk." She slapped his arm.

"Yea, well, there is that. Give me an hour and you will be hoppin' mad at me in no time."

A laugh escaped her lips and she reached up to dry her tears. "We'd better get movin'. I'm sure the kids are there already and we still need to pick up those hard hats."

Ben brought a hand to her face and met her green eyes. "If you need me, Ahawi, you find me. Does not matter if it's day or night. You hear?"

Maggie felt a small sense of belonging. *Why do I feel so safe with this man?* she wondered. She felt like she could stare into his warm brown eyes forever. A pain of regret filled her senses. Her feelings of betrayal weighed heavily on her chest. *What was wrong with her?*

"Thank you, Ben. Please tell Troy not to worry about me. I'll be fine," she said, walking over to the truck door. She got in and waited for him.

He smiled, shaking his head and pulling himself into the truck. The Suburban made its way down the two lane road, the smell of breakfast trailing behind them.

Chapter 9

*E*mpty food containers and paper plates lay strewn across the back of the Suburban.

Ellen took a sip of her coffee, sighing. "Thank you, Maggie! That was fantastic!"

"Yeah, thanks, Maggie," Alley chimed in.

Maggie put her orange juice down and smiled. "Well, thank Ben. He paid for it."

"No," Ben began in protest. "Maggie thought of you first. She had Troy up early this morning cooking. It's the thought that counts."

"Well, thank you both," Rick said, pushing his dark hair off of his face.

"You're welcome. I wanted you to start the day off right," Maggie said, going around the side of the Suburban. After opening the back door, she pulled out the hard hats.

"What are those?" Ellen questioned with a look of disgust.

"Well, it seems that they are going to start blasting sooner than expected. Ray called Ben with the news last night. We were instructed to wear these as a precaution," Maggie said, passing the hats around.

"But they're orange!" Ellen said in protest.

"Yes," Ben laughed, "they are easier to spot that way." He secured his on his head tightly and then helped Ellen and Alley adjust theirs.

Maggie looked at her watch, seeing that it was almost 8:30. The morning sun seemed warm to her, maybe too warm. Lord, how she hated the humidity. It always made the heat seem more oppressive. She raised her hand to shield her eyes from the sun, looking over the site. Her eye followed the site from the highway all the way up to the lush green of the ridge. Nervousness set in. The blasting starting early was not the best news she had heard. How were the five of them going to cross the distance before they had blasted up to them? She would just have to work longer days. She wouldn't make the kids stay longer; she would just pick up the slack herself.

"What is it, Maggie?" Rick asked.

Maggie blinked her green eyes and turned to face the group again. She took a deep breath. "Well, blasting early is not a good thing for us. We had a month originally, now who knows. I'm going to have to pull some longer days. May have to get some more help out here."

"Whatever you need, Maggie," Alley said.

"I will work the longer days, guys. There's no need to ruin your time here. This was not planned." She turned to Ben. "Do you have any plans tonight?"

He smiled at her, shaking his head. "No, not at all."

"How would you feel about camping out? I want to get up on that ridge and see what's there so I know where to place everyone on Monday."

"Sure. Sounds fun, actually."

"I'm game too, Maggie," Rick said with a smile.

"No, I want you guys to have a good weekend. Don't you have families to visit? Friends to see? You do know what fun is, don't you?" she smirked. Looking down, her mind mulled over Ben's words. Sounds fun actually...she could hear the anticipation he held in them. A feeling that, against her better judgement, she shared.

The three of them smiled. "Yes, I suppose we do," Rick said.

Maggie heard the faint hum of her cell phone vibrating against the seat of the truck. Rolling her eyes, she turned to Ben. "Can you get them started?"

"Sure, go ahead."

She opened the truck door, leaned over the seat, and picked

up her phone. Flipping it open, she said, "Hello?"

"How's my Maggie girl this morning? It's yer da'." His rough Scottish cadence caressed her ears.

She smiled at the sound of it. "Hello, da', how are you? How's Europe?"

"It's good. Wish ya would have come with me, Maggie girl."

"Me, too."

"Yer ma tells me that you've left again. She's worried about you, Mags, and so am I," he said, concern in his voice.

"Da' I'm fine. I promise. It's good to be working. They moved my deadline up this morning, so things are kind of in a crunch now."

"Well, I will na' keep ya then. Call me anytime, love, and please call yer ma when you get a chance."

"I will, da', promise."

"Aye, I love ya, Maggie girl. Ya make an old man proud."

Maggie smiled again. "I love you too, da'. Be safe."

After flipping the phone shut, she returned to the others. Ben had unpacked all of the tools and the kids were all digging. The first blast rang out and echoed throughout the site. Everyone jumped.

"It's going to be a long day," Maggie said with a laugh.

Ben handed her a brush and a trowel before following her down into the same trench they had been in the day before.

"Get your tools, Ben." She smiled. "If you're going to watch over us, you're going to work, and please bring me the camera while you're up there."

He winked at her and went to get another set of tools. "Here you go, Ahawi," he said, handing her the camera. He climbed down to meet her, then dug while she snapped some pictures.

The morning passed with little conversation. Both Rick and Alley found more arrowheads, but that seemed to be the extent of things. Numerous blasts filled the gaps between water breaks. Around lunchtime, they all piled into the Suburban and went back into to town in search of food. Ben had left them to eat while he ran a few errands and picked up some supplies for the evening. He joined up with them again before they headed back out to the site. As they pulled up, Maggie noticed an orange Roads Department truck and saw Ray get out of it, followed by another man. She parked the truck and everyone got out.

"Ray, how's the blasting going?" Ben questioned, his hand extended.

"We are actually on our way there now," Ray began, shaking Ben's hand. "Just wanted to stop by and check on you. How's it going?"

"Not much to report, really. Just some arrowheads," Maggie replied.

"Doctor Maggie Macleod, may I introduce my chief engineer on this project, George Harris."

The tall man held his hand out for her and she shook it. A large blast echoed again and Ray cursed under his breath. "Have they all been that loud?" he questioned.

Everyone said, "Yes!" in unison.

"They are using too much explosive," George said.

"Damn it! If I'm not there to babysit them every step of the way..." Ray trailed off, heading towards the truck again. He opened the door and looked their way. "Have a good weekend, guys."

"You too, Ray, and listen, Maggie and I are going to be camping out up on the ridge tonight. Just let your crew know," Ben hollered to him.

Ray nodded and the two men got into the truck, speeding down the highway.

The afternoon wore on with oppressive heat. Maggie's t-shirt was soaked with sweat and extremely uncomfortable. Standing up to stretch her back out, her gaze fell upon Ben and she couldn't help but notice that he had taken off both of his shirts, digging bare-chested. Wow! her mind all but sang. Shaking her head, Maggie tried to break the spell his half-naked, bronzed body seemed to hold over her. 'What the hell is happening to me?' In an effort to look at anything else but his smooth, sun-kissed skin, she turned her attention towards the kids and noticed them all knee-deep in the dirt.

The girls had the presence of mind to wear tank tops and Maggie felt herself wishing for one of her own. Wiping the sweat off of her brow had become somewhat of a habit for her, the humidity pressing down on them. In spite of the heat, though, they had all managed a steady pace, pushing the dig further south, much to her surprise. She was just about to call it a day when Rick let out a yell of excitement.

"Another arrowhead?" she called to him.

Rick stood up and it was hard to mistake the look of wonderment on his face. "No, I don't think so. You have to come see this!"

Everyone stopped what they were doing and quickly made their way over to him. Maggie looked down at the portion of the object he had uncovered and then looked up at them again. Thinking the sun was playing tricks on her, she looked down, trying to refocus.

"Am I seeing what I think I am?" Ben questioned.

Maggie got down on her hands and knees and took her brush to the object. She gently brushed away the years of sediment that clung to it. Looking up, she said, "Hand me a trowel." One was in her hand in seconds and she dug a little more of the object out.

"What is it, Maggie?" Ellen asked with excitement.

Maggie looked up at Ben with a smile. "It is what you think it is. I need the camera."

Ben turned and ran back to the truck. He returned in seconds with the camera. Maggie snapped off a few shots before getting up. "Well, guys, this is your first big discovery of the dig."

"More like ever," Alley snickered.

"Rick, congratulations. You have uncovered a mica mirror. They are very rare. Mica Mirrors were the first mineral mirrors known to man. They were used well before the Bronze Age. These are so rare, that are only a few left in the world. We have one at the Smithsonian and it is half the size that I think this one is."

Rick's enormous smile beamed at her and Maggie felt her spirits start to rise. This was the best part of her job—seeing the look of wonderment on the students' faces. She had discovered so many things that she sometimes forgot how good that felt. This was a wonderful moment.

"Way to go, Rick!" Ellen said, putting her arm around him.

"Ben, have you seen many of these?" Maggie questioned.

"There's one at the cultural center in Charleston and one at the college. I've never seen one like this. This is quite a thrill for me."

"It is wonderful, isn't it?" Alley questioned.

"We need to stake this off and then you guys can call it a day. Thanks for your efforts; it was a good day, guys! A good day indeed."

"We're not going to dig it out?" Rick asked, a little disappointed.

His enthusiasm brought another smile to her face. "Well, it will be here on Monday, Rick." She looked at her watch. "It's 4:30, don't you guys want to get going?"

"Not until we dig this out," they all said in unison.

"All right then. Let's get to it." Getting down on her knees, she picked up the trowel.

They all followed her to the dirt like it was second nature to them. Maggie giggled, feeling as euphoric as they did. This was why she had become a digger in the first place. The excitement of this moment was not lost on her.

"Now, the key is to be gentle. We don't know what kind of condition it's in below the surface and we don't want to chip it. You want to use your trowel, then your brush. Move the dirt and then brush it away." She followed the instructions. "See how that works?" Looking up at them, she handed the tools back to Rick. "This is your find, Rick; get to it."

It was almost 5:15 when Rick, followed by the two girls, carried their treasure over to the Suburban. Maggie and Ben sat on the tailgate watching them work, and now they fought the urge to laugh out loud. Rick was carrying the artifact like it had the plague, so afraid that he might damage it in some way. The girls acted like spotters of some sort. Holding their hands out under Rick's in the event that it slipped away.

"I had forgotten how great this is," Maggie whispered.

"How great what is?" Ben questioned.

"The excitement of new students. The wonderment of a first find. Look at them." She raised her hand towards the kids. "This has been such a great day for them."

"And you were a part of it, Maggie. You helped them experience this moment. You helped me. Teaching is not like this. I see things after you have unearthed them, it's not the same. I like being here and I just might love digging."

Maggie smiled back at him. Truth be told, she was starting to like him being there, too. Ben had been right, she had treated him badly yesterday. She felt regret for that because in truth, his presence had proved to be comforting to her in a short amount of time, and she couldn't forget that he had made her laugh. Really laugh. It had been so long since she had done that.

Rick stood before her, the small mirror, no bigger than the size of hishands. She met him with an approving gaze, reaching for a tarp and helping him wrap it. After answering his many questions about what would happen to it, she and Ben bid the kids well, wishing them a good weekend, something that seemed to be a possibility for Maggie, herself. The ridge awaited her and her newfound partner. That was a thought that made her smile.

Chapter 10

*M*aggie pulled the Suburban off the highway at the dig site, parking in her usual spot. The evening sun was hanging low in the sky, casting beautiful shades of pink mixed with orange. It's so striking, Maggie thought. What was more beautiful, though, was the breeze that had begun to blow. Dogwood blossoms floated on the air and the newly green trees swayed as if in a dance.

Maggie got out of the truck and leaned against it, taking in the spectacular view. She had traveled most of the world, called one of the most metropolitan cities in the states her home, but she had never seen country like this before. Coming here was a means to an end. It never occurred to her that she would fall in love with its beauty. No matter where she looked, she could find something to like. From the old abandoned industry buildings, to the barges sailing down the river, even the soft moss that grew up many of the trees. It was all so pretty, grabbing her attention, filling her senses.

Looking down at her watch, she wondered where Ben was. They had parted ways at the Inn and he had agreed to meet her back at the site at 6:30. She'd had just enough time to shower, change, as well as pack a small bag before returning. Ben had assured her that he had picked up everything they would need for the evening; she just needed to bring herself. It was now 6:45 she noticed, looking at her watch. Her new partner was nowhere in sight.

After opening the truck door, she leaned across the seat for her camera. The whole point of this little "camp out" was to map out a plan for the crew. Now that the blasting had begun, the pressure was really on. She was about fifty feet from the truck when she heard another vehicle pull up. Turning, she saw Ben get out of his truck and walk towards her with a welcoming grin.

"I'd almost given up on you," she called to him.

"As I said, Ahawi, to know me is to love me. Have you been waiting long?"

"No, not really. It gave me a chance to appreciate the scenery. It's quite a beautiful night."

Ben nodded in agreement, looking around the view that lay before them. He found that his gaze quickly returned to her, though. Suddenly, he was fighting the overwhelming urge to gasp. The sun was hanging low behind her head and the gentle breeze picked up her auburn curls, blowing them softly around her beautiful face. She reached up for her sunglasses, pushing them to the top of her head in an effort to tame her tresses. Her eyes were like two deep, beautifully cut emeralds. He could see no beginning and no end in them. They just simply grabbed a person's attention and wouldn't let go. He was beginning to think that he could find a home with her. That was a possibility he wanted to explore to the fullest.

"Ben," she called to him.

He shook his head and the spell was broken. "Sorry, I was just thinking about Rick's find today. That was sure something, wasn't it?"

"Yes, it was, and he was so excited. Like I said, I've missed that. I've been too pre-occupied on my digs to notice the little things. You know?"

"Well, seeing the smile on your face now is sure something, too. You came to the land of the rednecks and found something you lost. That's a pretty good thing in my book."

Maggie burst out laughing. It was a beautiful sound.

Ben let out a chuckle himself. Her laugh seemed infectious to him.

"Now how did you know what I was thinking?" she questioned, her green eyes shining.

"It's West Virginia. Everyone has thought that a time or two. A person only needs to spend time here, and their minds change."

"I suppose so, Ben. This time of year is quite lovely."

Ben nodded, agreeing with her. He made his way to the back of his truck and started unpacking the gear he had brought. With a smile, Maggie went to the Suburban and threw a large backpack over her shoulder before heading over to Ben. He met her glance, a little surprised.

"I know you said you had everything, Ben, but I am not a 'wee woman' and packing for outings is one of the things I do well. There's even a tent in here." She patted her pack gently.

Smiling, he winked back at her. Maggie liked that. Liked the way the sun sparkled in his warm brown eyes, and, in that moment, it didn't matter why. Ben threw his large pack over his shoulder and closed the tail gate on his truck.

"No one accused you of being a 'wee woman', Ahawi, but just to be on the safe side, maybe you should lead the way. After all, you are the lead on this project."

Maggie raised her eyebrows at the challenge. What was it about this man? He seemed to know every button that she had and exactly how to push them. He was grinning at her in an effort to spur her on.

"Aye," she began, her accent thick. "Maybe I should." A giggle escaped her lips before she turned and headed for the ridge.

Ben followed, wondering just what this night had in store for them. He felt something in his bones. Something big was coming their way and he knew that his grandfather had felt it long before he did. His glance returned to Maggie and a whistle escaped him. She had been right; the scenery was quite stunning tonight.

Chapter 11

"How does this look?" asked Ben, looking down at the Ohio River. It was a fantastic view with the town of New Martinsville north and looking over a length of the river all the way south.

"Looks a little close to the cliff to me," Maggie laughed.

"Well I didn't mean right here, I meant...back here," Ben answered. He walked ten paces back from the edge.

Maggie studied the area, nodding in approval. "Okay, it'll do, I suppose," she smirked with a wink. They dropped their gear at their feet and started to unpack. Ben watched Maggie remove a tent from her bags, then kick rocks and sticks away for a clear base. He then took his tent out, which had been haphazardly packed, and fumbled trying to find the corners. Searching for a rock to drive the stakes, he looked up to see Maggie unzip the screen and crawl inside with her sleeping bag.

"Damn! How did you do that so fast?" he said, peeking in the door.

Maggie stopped what she was doing and looked at him. "Oh...it's a throw up. You just...throw it up." Ben just shook his head, going back to work.

He took his Bowie knife, cut two center posts for his tent, and whittled them to the right size.

Maggie smiled when she saw him. "Did you lose your poles or something?" she asked.

"Yeah, well..." Ben laughed. "We took a keg up this holler one time, me and about thirty other people, and the harder it rained the drunker we wanted to get, and before long they bet me that I couldn't...well, yeah, I lost them."

"Ah," Maggie said, laughing. "No keg this trip, huh?"

"That was back in the day. Back when I could do that and still get up before noon."

Once his tent was up, Ben cleared the ground in a large circle for a fire between the tents. He gathered firewood as Maggie unfolded a small table and laid out some equipment. By the time he returned with a third arm-full, Maggie was sitting cross-legged on the ground talking on her cell phone.

"Good. No, just the first night I was here. Since then it's been sunny, hot and muggy, actually...we're camping out tonight... me and my crew...yes. Oh, could you check the weather for me on the internet real quick? New Martinsville. Okay, I'll plan for that, then. Okay, I have to go...I will, Collin, I promise...love you too... goodnight."

Ben sat down and carefully placed twigs over a paper, lighting them to nurse the fire. Dusk had fallen as Maggie walked to the edge of the cliff, looking out at the distant lights of the town, a truly stunning sight to behold. The deep purples of evening twilight wrapped around the soft glow of the far-away lights, as if wrapping New Martinsville in velvet for the evening. "It must have been so much different centuries ago. No towns, maybe the dim light of a fire, canoes and flatboats instead of diesel engines." She then walked back to where the flames of the fire were growing and Ben was putting on bigger twigs.

"My grandfather always says, 'White man builds big fire and sits way back,'" Ben said with a smile, "I'm real hungry." He piled the wood on thick, then took out his knife and whittled roasting poles.

"What did he say about big knives?" Maggie asked.

"This?" Ben held out the ten-inch blade. "This looks pretty small to a bear or a bobcat that wants your food."

"I see," Maggie said, folding her arms, "so it's not just something to prop up a male ego, having a big knife?"

"Nope."

"Are there many bears around?" "No, not many. Probably

72

no more than a couple close enough to smell us," Ben said with a smile.

"And so we're cooking?"

"Yes, we are. Here, here's you a pole. You might want to fire that first. It will be a while before we have hot coals anyway."

Maggie watched Ben, placing her stick close to the flames beside his. She watched the firelight cast shadows across Ben's noble features. His wonderfully warm brown eyes weren't the only thing that seemed to endear him to her. The angular line of his nose...his strong chin. He was beautiful and quite a contrast of rugged versus warmth. "Let me ask you, Ben, do you think we'll find anything else here? I mean, I'm just wondering why the council felt so strongly about sending you here to watch over me. Was this area a sacred place to them? This dig came up so fast, that I wasn't able to complete proper research of the area beforehand."

"My grandfather seemed to be concerned when he told me about this, so I suppose we might. He didn't get specific, but I have to believe he's concerned about burial grounds, things like that."

"Well, I can assure you, anything of that nature will be treated with care and respect."

"Oh, I know, but you have to realize, what's considered respectful to some people could be a real slap in the face to others."

"I'm sure," Maggie replied, hoping that along the way Ben would gain confidence in her sensitivity for other cultures. "So what does your grandfather think of all the industry?" Maggie asked, pointing to the steam rising from the plants just to the north. "I'm sure he's seen a lot of changes in his life, the way we treat the earth and all."

"It's better now than it was when he was younger. Companies do a good job in general because I think they see value in it. Not like in the early part of the 20th century when the state was raped by oil and coal companies. Some of the older people don't care for change much, but he's pretty accepting."

"Does he live close by?"

"Less than an hour away. I can't get him closer. That's where he's less accepting," Ben laughed. "This county, Wetzel, was named for the infamous Indian killer, Lewis Wetzel."

"Yes, I saw that," Maggie replied. "He was a frontier hero of sorts..."

"He was a hero to some, like the people who named the county after him, but really he was a sad product of the hatred of men. I can understand...anyone can understand a man who fights for his family, his land. Lewis Wetzel lived his life on a mission to kill anyone who wasn't white. Not exactly Daniel Boone. Tribes like the Delaware would send peace emissaries to talk to the white man and even though they had been promised safe passage, he would attack them and kill them, as publicly and cruelly as possible. You see, he was fueled by the adoration of some other 'frontiersmen'. He was said to have murdered dozens. Then in 1788 he was hired by the US Military as a scout down in Marietta at Fort Harmar. Which ironically had been constructed and manned with American military to protect the Delaware from incursions by whites from south of the River. Tegunteh, the great Seneca leader, was sent there to finish a treaty, which he had long worked for, and one that would mean peace for the people. On the way to the talks, Wetzel ambushed and killed Tegunteh. Now that's an inability to accept change."

The two sat in silence for a time, then Maggie asked, "Isn't this fire ready yet?"

"If it isn't, too bad, because I'm starved!" Ben said, tearing open the package. He put two hotdogs on his stick then passed the bag to Maggie. The fire crackled as the hotdogs cooked and darkness engulfed them. The two did not talk about the task at hand but about family, hobbies, and about how the smoke seemed to eventually chase them no matter on which side they sat.

Chapter 12

*M*aggie woke up with a start, for no other reason than the heaviness of the air. To say that one could cut it with a knife would be an understatement. She sat up, pushing her damp curls off of her face and looking out the screen door of her tent. A thick fog had rolled in and blanketed the campsite with moisture. In her state of semi-consciousness, she soon realized that shoving her sleeping bag down to her feet made no difference. It was a typical muggy night in the Ohio Valley. Looking out, she could see Ben fast asleep by the still flickering firelight. She looked at her watch to see that it was only 3 AM. Rolling over with the intention of getting more sleep, she realized that would be impossible until she answered the call of nature. Wrinkling her brow, she cursed her luck. Damn my tiny bladder. Venturing out into this scene was not her idea of a good time. Carefully unzipping her door as to not wake Ben, she grabbed a flashlight, slipped on her hiking boots without tying the laces, and walked softly down the hill. After what she considered an appropriate distance, she unbuttoned her shorts and squatted down. A rustling in the bushes made her jump. Please don't be a snake! She turned on the flashlight, shining it frantically at the ground in front of her.

"Come on, come on!" she said to hurry herself, the noise getting closer. She stood up, pulling her shorts on quickly. Whatever it was crept closer by the second. Maggie turned cautiously, feeling wet leaves of the low hanging branches against her skin. As dark as it was and with all the fog, she briefly thought this was a good set up for a horror movie. The rustling grew closer and she picked up her pace, hoping she would not have to call out for Ben to save her. She jogged until the flicker of a fire could be seen at a distance. It was to her right, indicating she was only a few paces off her original path. A large flat rock sat in her way, but Maggie decided to step over it when her feet slipped out from under her. She screamed loudly as she fell. Her seat hit the rock hard and she slid several feet down. Once she came to a stop, she rocked back hitting her head on the solid rock behind her. In a few seconds it was over, but Maggie was in a lot of pain. Her ears were ringing and a rush of blood to her head made her too faint to call out again. Blotchy black spots filled her vision and she fought overwhelmingly to gain control of her senses. If she didn't, she knew that she would pass out and then no one would find her.

Gathering herself as best she could, Maggie realized she was in trouble. She had fallen down a crevice and could see nothing. She had dropped the flashlight in the fall and now grappled in a vain attempt to locate it. Finally she gained the strength to call out, "Ben! Help me!" An intense pain ran through her head and she grabbed it in agony. She took a few more minutes to gather her strength while fighting off the urge to just lie down and close her eyes. Calling out again. "Ben! Help! Help me damn it!" Tears blurred her vision.

"Maggie!" she heard faintly from above. "Maggie, where are you?"

"Here! I fell down here!"

"Ahawi, keep talking. I can hear you!" Ben yelled. She could catch glimpses of a flashlight above her.

"Ben! I'm down here. I hit my head, and it hurts...so bad." Maggie heard the trembling in her voice. She shivered, feeling like she could fall apart at any moment. Just then leaves and dirt streamed down on her. Ben was standing at the edge of the drop looking down at her.

"Maggie! Don't move!" Ben called, the flashlight illuminating her face.

"Who's moving?" she cried out in aggravation.

"Don't move a muscle; there's no telling how far you would

fall. You stay right where you are while I get a rope." Maggie heard Ben run through the grass. Heard his footsteps recede only to return a few minutes later. He was breathing heavily. "Maggie, I'm here. I'll be down in a minute." He tied off one end of the rope to a tree before shining the light down the hole again. Maggie had fallen down a steep rock face of about forty-five degrees. She was more than ten feet below, sitting with her legs under her, along with a layer of leaves and dirt.

"Be careful!" Maggie whimpered as Ben repelled down the slope.

"Maggie, how did you get down here?"

"I was walking back to my tent and I slid down." Ben was now sitting beside her, examining her with a flashlight.

"What the hell were you doing in the woods in the middle of the night?"

"I had to pee, okay?"

"Down here?"

"No! I walked out here to pee and then was on my way back."

"Well, shit, Maggie, why didn't you just pee behind your tent?"

"Because you were out there by the fire. Ouch! Careful," Maggie said when Ben found the knot on the back of her head.

"Oh, and I was gonna look?"

"I have a bashful bladder!"

"You have a big knot back here. Let me see you," Ben said. He shined the light in her eyes. "I don't know, you might have a concussion. How do you feel?"

"I feel okay. My head hurts a little. Let me stand up."

"No! Let's just sit here and rest for a second before we get you out of here." Ben moved the Flashlight in an arch around them, illuminating their surroundings. They were in a cave, with smooth walls and a low ceiling where they sat. The light would not reveal below the shelf they sat on, as it was too deep. "Hey, Ahawi," Ben said as surprised as he knew she would be, "you could have just used those steps over there."

Maggie looked to their right in awe. There were indeed steps, rounded and ragged, but steps nonetheless. Ben tried to stand up but bumped his head on the ceiling above. "Careful," Maggie said, rising to her knees and moving to her right.

"Hey, just sit back down," Ben said, but it was a wasted breath. Maggie grabbed the light from his hands. The ceiling opened to their right and Maggie was now on her feet and walking toward the set of steps, about four feet wide and leading down into the darkness.

"Holy shit! Are these really here?"

"Yes, they are, Ben. Yes they are." Maggie examined them, running her hands over the pitted stone like picking out fruit at a market. "They are steps and they are manmade."

"Someone carved a set of stairs into the rock here?"

"Nope. These are all individual stones," Maggie said, squinting to see the seams. She shone the light down until it struck a floor. "Come on."

"Now don't be stupid. You have a head injury and you need to go to the emergency room," Ben tugged at her sleeve.

"Ben, you have two choices. You can go down here with me, or wait here for me. Either works, so suit yourself." With that, Maggie started descending the stairs with Ben holding her back belt loop with one hand and the rope with the other. "Look! Look, look, look!" Maggie squealed, shining the light all around as the two reached a large room. The sandstone dimly reflected enough light to reveal walls that had been covered completely with drawings. Some areas were painted with red, black, and white, with heavy signs of the minerals from water encrusting them.

"You feel okay?" Ben asked, listening to Maggie pant.

"I'm fine. Hey...hey listen...you hear that?"

"I must not. What do you hear?"

"The acoustics of this room. Does this sound like any cave you've been in?" Maggie questioned.

"No...no it doesn't. The sound is dead, there's no echo at all. So what does that mean, other than it would be a great place for a recording studio?"

"I'm betting it's by design," Maggie responded. She approached the far wall, feeling the musty air sitting in her lungs. Dust fell from all the movement. She shined her light across the surface, revealing more drawings. "Someone put a lot of work into this, Ben."

"Who? I mean, the drawings don't look Cherokee to me."

"I don't know, but there's enough here to find out, that's for sure! Look, see this? Every few feet, just about eye level, there are holes carved out, maybe for lighting, like torches or something."

"I keep looking to see a still," Ben said with a laugh.

"No one has been here for a long time. Look at the floor. There are no prints other than ours." As she spoke, Maggie gently brushed away some of the dirt from the floor, revealing a mosaic pattern. "This floor isn't sandstone. It's been inlayed with...crystalline-type stones. This looks like quartz," Maggie said, dropping to her knees for a closer look. "This is beautiful. Absolutely beautiful." She then rose to her feet, but quickly dropped again, and this time not on purpose.

"Ahawi!" Ben yelled, catching her. "Okay, that's it, we're leaving."

"No, I'm fine," Maggie said faintly.

"Like hell you are! Now I'm giving you two choices. You can come out of here walking or hog- tied," Ben said, putting his arm around Maggie's waist and leading her back to the steps. They ascended to the top where they noticed the steps lead up to a large rock that blocked the original entrance to the cave. They continued on, using the rope to scale the incline they had descended earlier. It was still dark out and Maggie felt across the ground to find the light she had dropped.

"What are you doing?" Ben asked.

"I'm looking for my flashlight. The batteries must have jarred loose when I dropped it."

"We can look for it tomorrow, or when you're feeling better."

"But I want to mark this somehow, and forget tomorrow, we're coming back later today!"

"Well, we'll string the rope back to the tents then. Now come on, let's get off this hill."

"So what happens when some kid comes along and falls down the hole?"

"Maggie, no kids are going to be up here, and if they do, a four-wheeler will never fit down that hole."

"Ben, I'm serious. Now look around for a flat rock big enough to cover it," Maggie said, looking around where she could see at her feet.

"Hey, why don't I just leave the rope down the hole for them? That way..."

"No one is going to get hurt on my account!" Maggie said adamantly.

Ben must have known that he sounded insensitive, since she couldn't get him to make eye contact. He turned to grab a piece of dead wood. It was just long enough to fit across the hole in a manner that would keep someone from stepping into it. "How's that?" he asked.

"That's good," said Maggie after examining the opening. "Now we can go."

Ben allowed Maggie to take the flashlight from his hand and lead the way back to camp. By the time they got off the hill it was daylight, and Maggie convinced Ben that all she needed was a few hours of rest back at the Inn.

Chapter 13

*H*er eyes opened and Maggie saw nothing but darkness. Eyelids closed again, heavy with ache. She wanted to slip back down into sleep, to let the velvet darkness wrap around her, but her mind wouldn't allow it. Flashes of her falling down a cliff embankment filled her mind and her eyes opened once again. She winced as the pain came to her in short stabs. Gasping, Maggie sat up and instantly grabbed her head.

"Damn it!" she cursed.

The lamp across the room came on and soft light flooded her sight. Blinking her eyes closed, she struggled to focus. Why is everything so blurry? she wondered. A hand squeezed her bare shoulder and she jumped. Pain shot through her.

"Oh!" she cried.

"Easy, Ahawi," the voice came to her, caressing her ears just as his strong hands did her shoulders.

Maggie did not fight the touch. She let herself fall back into his arms. He sat on the bed, still holding her. "You gave me quite a scare." Maggie squeezed her eyes shut. "Just relax. You are safe now." He wrapped his arms around her tightly and Maggie took a deep breath. This felt like home. Being in his arms felt safe. How could that be?

"What happened?" The words came out, but her throat was dry and she didn't sound like herself. Opening her eyes again, she was met with Ben's warm gaze. There was a look of concern in his large brown eyes.

He reached down, gently brushing her auburn curls off of her face. "You fell. Don't you remember? You have a minor concussion."

"Vaguely."

As if sensing her discomfort, Ben reached over and grabbed a glass of water that sat on the bedside table. Raising her slightly, he brought it to her lips gently. Taking a sip, the cold water soothed her.

"That's it."

Maggie took another sip before he took the glass away, setting it back on the table.

"I fell...down the embankment," she whispered.

"Yes. The doc says nothing's broken, but you do have a large bump on your head and some cuts and bruises."

"The doc?" Maggie questioned, looking around the room. They were in her room at the Inn. She looked down at herself. She remembered she had been wearing a pair of shorts and a t-shirt. She was in her green, silk chemise now. How had that happened?

"Well, we are in a small town. He came to you, but enough of this, you need to rest, Ahawi," he said softly. Maggie closed her eyes, feeling warm tears on her face; she reached for his hand, clasping it tightly.

"He didn't happen to give me anything for the pain, did he?"

Ben's grip tightened on her hand. "I can't get it until the pharmacy opens in the morning. He gave you a shot of something before he left, though. You've been asleep for hours."

"Well, it's not helping anymore."

"Grandfather brought over some willow bark tea. It will help with the pain and help you get back to sleep." He laid her back to the pillows gently before standing up.

Maggie reached for him, taking his hand in hers in desperation. She fought the pain and whispered, "Ben."

He turned and met her green eyes.

"Please, do na' leave me." Her words came out in a breathy whisper.

Smiling, he leaned down and kissed her brow gently. "I won't leave, Ahawi, someone has to make sure you get rest." He pulled back and winked at her.

"I can na' stay in bed! We're on a deadline, and after what we found this morning, how can ya say that? It was this morning, wasn't it?"

"As I said, someone has to make sure you rest." He walked over to the vanity, reaching for a thermos sitting there. "I called Dr. Altman. She's on her way out as well as one of your brothers. Everyone is quite excited about your find."

Maggie brought her hands to her face, fighting more tears. Why am I so emotional? she wondered. "Which one?"

"What?" he questioned, a mug in his hand.

"Which one of my brothers is coming?" Ben sat down next to her again and helped prop her up against the cherry headboard of the sleigh bed. He handed her the mug. "Drink. It will help, I promise."

Reluctantly, Maggie took a sip. To her surprise, it tasted like normal herbal tea. It had a soothing quality to it. The aroma that filled her senses was calming too. She would have sworn it was chamomile or jasmine.

"Dr. Altman said that Collin was on his way. She thought he would be of some help. Are your brothers diggers, too?"

Maggie took another sip. "This is amazing, Ben. What's in here?"

"Willow bark. My people have been using it for pain and fever relief forever. Your doctors don't recognize our medicines, though. Grandfather will be pleased that you like it." He smiled at her.

"My two youngest brothers are diggers. Collin, my older brother, is a chemical engineer and a botanist. He'll be able to identify the plant matter we'll surely find in the cave. I was actually hoping I could persuade your grandfather to come in and help decipher the writings we found." She took another sip of the tea, feeling more relaxed.

"I'm sure he'd like that. He says that you have a great spirit."

"I'm looking forward to meeting him," she said, yawning.

Ben reached over and took the mug from her. "I think that's enough for now. Why don't you close your eyes and rest for a while? I'll be over on the sofa if you need anything, and don't try to get up without help. The doc said the bump on your head will cause you to be unsteady. I promise in the morning I'll go for your prescription."

"Actually, I don't think I need it. The tea has helped tremendously."

Standing up, he reached for the covers and pulled them tight around her. "Rest, Ahawi."

She watched him walk over to the cream floral sofa. He took his shoes off before he unbuttoned his denim work shirt. As hard as Maggie tried, she could not look away. He finished with the buttons and he let the shirt slide down his muscled arms. His tan back was perfect, almost as if it was chiseled out of marble. As he turned, she noticed that his chest was the same way—muscular, tan, and perfect in every way. He reached up for the tie that was holding his dark hair back and took it out. Raven hair spilled over his shoulders and Maggie fought the urge to gasp. His hair was so black she could see blue in it and she knew it would be the softest thing she would ever touch if she only got the chance.

"Ben," she said, taking a deep breath. He turned and met her with a smile.

"Yes?" Her eyes took in the sight of him. Had he always been this breathtaking or was the tea playing tricks on her? "Why don't you call me Maggie? Why do you call me 'Ahawi'?"

He smiled again. "Because you are like the Ahawi, the deer. Beautiful, delicate, always running away, always exploring, and never realizing how fragile you truly are. I think it suits you better than Maggie."

Maggie smiled at the thought of that. He seemed to know her so well already. She wondered how that could be, wondered why she felt so safe with him. It was something she could not control, even though she tried.

"And 'Sahale'? What does it mean?"

He walked across the room to the cherry footboard of the bed. "Sahale is the falcon above. A truly free spirit, not bound by all of this," he said, holding his arms up and motioning to the room.

"Walls cannot hold him," she whispered.

"No. He can have a master, but he will always remain truly free."

"I like that. It suits you better than Ben. May I call you Sahale?"

He smiled again, his face softening. Maggie swore that his brown eyes grew larger, and for a moment she felt she could see nothing but open sky lit by tiny stars. She felt true freedom and wished she could fall into that beautiful night sky. He blinked and the illusion faded.

"What did you see, Ahawi?" he questioned, his voice low.

"What's in that tea?" She squeezed her eyes shut.

"What did you see?" he questioned again, this time more insistent.

Opening her eyes, Maggie met his glance. "I saw the most beautiful night sky I have ever seen. It was lit with tiny stars..." She stopped, thinking she sounded crazy.

"Grandfather was right," he whispered. "You may call me Sahale if you so wish it."

"I wish it."

He nodded and walked back over to the couch. "Rest," he said, lying down. "Morning will be here sooner than you think."

Maggie smiled, closing her eyes. She gave herself up to the feeling of sleep. It took her softly to peaceful depths she hadn't known in six months.

Chapter 14

*M*aggie sat at a table in front of large plate glass windows, waiting for her oatmeal to come. Even with her sunglasses on she felt the light was an almost overpowering strain on her senses. The night had passed too quickly for her. She had rested for most of it and Ben sat up with her in the moments when nightfall faded and gave way to morning twilight. As promised, he'd helped her get dressed and to the restaurant downstairs before heading over to get her prescription. She'd taken it upon herself to order breakfast for him and was now sipping on some of the tea he'd given her the night before.

A loud rattle rose up from the table, startling her. Quickly, she reached for her cell phone and flipped it open.

"Hello?" Her voice sounded hushed...a little weary.

"Maggie girl, its Ma'. Are you all right? Collin called to tell me what happened." Rachel's warm accent caressed Maggie's ear.

"Ma...," Maggie said in protest, rolling her eyes.

"Should I come out there? Do you need to come home?"

"Ma!" Maggie was more persistent this time, but to no avail.

"I'm just so worried about ya', Maggie. Collin said that you hit yer head."

Maggie took a deep breath and let it out slowly. "Ma, I'm fine. I promise. I have a minor concussion and some bruises. The doctor gave me the 'all clear'."

"Do you need me?" Her mother's voice pleaded with her from the other end.

"Thank you, Ma, but I'll be fine. Collin should be here soon and everyone here is so nice. I'm in good hands and I'm going to be fine. Trust me, please. If there are any changes, I'll have Collin call you right away."

"Yer sure, Margaret?" "Yes, Ma, I'm sure." "All right, then. I will leave ya to yer work. Yer

Da' has asked me to join him; I'll probably leave tomorrow."

"You should, Ma. Have some fun and don't worry about me."

"I always worry about you kids. My job, ya know." Rachel's voice always seemed to put her at ease. How she loved to hear her mother speak.

Maggie smiled. "I ken, Ma. I love ya, and kiss Da' for me," she answered, her own accent thick.

"I love ya, Maggie girl!"

Smiling, Maggie flipped the phone closed and looked out the window again. The day had the makings of perfection—warm sunlight, blue sky, and soft white clouds. She hoped she could cope with the humidity better today by wearing a pair of shorts and a tank top. Blinking, she caught sight of Ben crossing the street back to the Inn. His tan work shirt looked unbearably stretched across the chiseled muscle of his chest. She blinked again, thinking he wouldn't look as good, but she was wrong. His wranglers looked like they had been poured on to his body. 'Wonder what kind of underwear he has on?' She shook her head gently, her stare never wavering. Is there any light that this man does not look good in? He'd been so nice to her last night, had taken good care of her, and most of all, had managed to keep her fears at bay. She didn't know what was really happening to her; didn't really want to think about the way she was beginning to feel about him. It was just there. Any time she saw him, it was there and she didn't know what she was going to do about it.

Troy appeared and set breakfast down in front of her as Ben's steps fell on the hardwood.

"Can I get you anything else, Maggie?" Troy asked, concern in his voice.

"No, this should do, Troy. Thank you."

"Well, I'm just in time, I see," Ben said, rounding the corner to the table.

"I didn't know what you'd like. I hope this is okay?"

"I will eat almost anything, Ahawi. Thank you for ordering for me."

Maggie smiled and stared down at her oatmeal.

"Let me know if you need anything else," Troy replied before he headed back to the kitchen.

Ben mixed his eggs and potatoes together and then added a large helping of salsa. Maggie felt a little queasy and brought her hand to her mouth. "Maggie, are you okay?"

She took a deep breath and swallowed hard. "Yes, I'm fine. My stomach is just a little upset this morning. I'm sure it will pass."

"That's to be expected with a head injury. The oatmeal will do you good." Ben set his fork down and reached out to clasp Maggie's hand. She didn't fight it.

"I think you should rest when we're through here. We can head out to the site later this afternoon after your brother gets here."

Much to her surprise, Maggie agreed. She just wanted to rest her eyes for a while. Looking up, she met his warm glance. "I think that would be good. Thank you. Be..." She stopped herself, looking down, remembering their conversation from the night before. "Sahale. Thank you for taking care of me."

"It's my pleasure, Ahawi."

Maggie smiled at him in return. Suddenly an uncomfortable feeling swept over her. Ben's stare was unnerving. She couldn't put her finger on why, but she started to feel like he wanted to devour her. Make her a meal of sorts. It had been a very long time since a man had looked at her that way. She felt a bit excited by it...panicked even. Whatever was going to happen in this moment would change everything. She just knew it, and looking into his beautiful eyes told her that he knew it too. Letting go of her hand, he reached over, tilted her chin up and took her sunglasses off so he could see her deep green eyes. They sat there for a few moments, staring at each other.

Maggie found that she could not tear herself from his stare. She couldn't even blink. He's not going to do it, is he? her mind was screaming, and what was worse was the fact that she thought she wanted him to do it. She watched him part his lips and run his tongue over them.

He inched slowly towards her, their eyes clearly fixed on each other. Taking a deep breath, Maggie closed them and felt the softness of his warm lips as he pressed them gently to hers. The hair stood up on the back of her neck when he pressed further into her and parted his lips. Maggie opened herself to him, their tongues mingling softly. How can this be? He feels like home, she thought. He brought his hands to her face, cupping it gently. The kiss grew deeper and the thought of it ending pained her.

"Well, I see that you are in good hands." The voice came from behind them.

Both she and Ben startled apart and turned to look in the direction of the voice. Her brother's eyes met hers, as well as Bev's. They both had little grins on their faces. "Hello, Mags. How are you?" Collin questioned with raised eyebrows.

Maggie quickly pulled away from Ben's grasp and blinked. She found she had no words.

Collin laughed and crossed the distance between them. Bev followed suit.

"Might we join you?"

Maggie stood up and embraced her brother with a flushed face. "Yes, of course you can." She hugged Bev and then motioned for them to sit. "This is Ben Adams. He is representing the Elder Council of the ANAWV. He's here to represent the interests of the elders on the council."

Ben stood up and extended a hand to Collin, then to Bev. They all exchanged pleasantries as everyone took their seats. Collin met his sister's glance again, sensing fear in her. He reached over and took her hand, holding it tightly. "It's good to see you, Mags."

"You too," Maggie replied.

"How are you? What did the doctor say? Shouldn't you be at the hospital?"

Maggie held her hand up to try and hold him off. "I'm fine, Collin. The doctor said that I have a mild concussion, but he gave me some medication and I got some good rest last night, thanks to Ben and his grandfather. I won't lie, I'm a little sore, but nothing is going to keep me from going back out there today. There's so much for us to do."

"Fair enough, but I don't think a little rest first would hurt you."

Ben chuckled. "I've been trying to tell her that all morning. Have you any idea how hard it was to get her back here and keep her here?"

"A task I know well, my friend," Collin said with a smile. "You had your work cut out for ya, that's for sure."

"Did you have to tie her down?" Bev asked with a grin.

Ben burst out laughing and Maggie felt her checks flush.

"All right, you've all had yer fun! Once ya see what we found, you'll wonder how I could've left it in the first place."

Troy emerged from the kitchen and quickly placed menus in front of the two new comers.

"Just shout when you're ready to order. I'm going to go make sure everything's in place for your stay here. So glad that you'll be joining us."

They all agreed and watched him leave the room. An uneasy silence fell over the small table and it was enough to make Maggie squirm. What had she gotten herself into?

Chapter 15

After finishing a somewhat awkward breakfast, Maggie now found herself sitting on the sofa in her room. Collin sat across from her with an enormous grin on his face, the sunlight from the windows shining on his tightly cropped auburn hair. Ben had invited Bev to ride with him to his grandfather's and she had accepted, leaving the two siblings alone. Oh, how Maggie wished that she was the one who was invited.

Michael and Collin had been close. As close as any brothers could be, and now, a short six months later, Collin walked in and found her kissing someone else. How on earth can I explain that to him? She took a deep breath and covered her face with her hands.

"Perhaps you should lay down, Mags," Collin said softly, interrupting her deep thoughts.

"I'm fine."

"That's funny, because ya' do na' look fine to me," his accent flared.

"Can we just get this over with Collin?" she said in exasperation.

"Whatever are you referring to, sister of mine?" His green eyes held a hint of mischief.

Maggie dropped her hands with a sigh. "Col, please! I'm na' in the mood. All I can say is I'm sorry."

Collin reached over and pulled her to him, tucking her close to his side. "Mags, yer my little sis. All I want is for ya' to be happy. Ben seems like a nice guy."

He is, she thought. He really is.

"All me and the boys want is for ya' to be happy. It's been long enough."

Maggie felt a swell of emotion come to her. Tears escaped her long lashes and fell warm on her face. "But, you loved Michael..."

"I did, Mags," he soothed, "and so did you."

"I still do," she said in a hushed voice.

"Michael would want you to be happy. He will always be with ya', but he would never want ya to live yer life alone. Find some happiness."

Maggie pulled back and met her brother's gaze. "I've tried to stop this, Col. I really have, but there's just something about Ben. He drives me crazy and I hate him half of the time, but he's wonderful."

"And you like him, Mags. That is all that matters. No one is questioning yer feelings for Michael. We all know you loved him. The fact that picture is sitting over there is proof," he said, pointing to the photo on the bedside table. "Give yerself a break. You've hurt enough. Do na' deny yerself some happiness."

Maggie put her arms around her brother tightly. "Aye, yer a good lad, Collin."

"I love ya, little sister. Now go lay down. I'll wake ya when they get back and we'll go explore yer find."

Maggie agreed. She knew that she could use a little shut eye. Hugging her brother, she walked him to the door. He kissed her before closing the door behind him. Kicking her shoes off, she crossed the room to the sleigh bed and sat down. A smile came to her lips as her mind returned to Ben. Her eyes settled on the photo. Michael had been the love of her life and until this moment she never expected to love anyone else. Was Collin right? Had it been long enough? She lay back against the large, soft pillows. Whatever the answer was, Maggie really wanted to find out. Ben had come into her life like a breath of fresh air. Everyone needed fresh air, needed it to survive. Maggie closed her eyes with a smile again and let sleep take her as the early afternoon sunlight cast shadows across the floor.

Chapter 16

The knock became more persistent, followed by the loud buzz of her cell phone. Maggie struggled to open her eyes, to shake off the haze of deep sleep. Blinking, she noticed that the early afternoon sunlight had given way to evening twilight. "Damn!" she whispered, sitting up slowly. The knocks kept growing louder and her cell phone had buzzed itself right off of the bedside table and onto the floor. Holding her head, she stood up and walked over to the door.

"Maggie!" the voice called to her.

"Hold on, I'm coming!" Holding the wall, she braced herself against the doorway and reached for the knob. Turning it slowly, it gave way. The whole gang stood before her, even the kids. Maggie felt a little woozy and reached back for the wall. Ben walked in and picked her up, taking her back over to the bed.

"It's okay, Ahawi. I've got you," he whispered.

"What's going on? You all told me to get some rest."

He smiled down at her as everyone came into the room. "We did, but you've been out for quite a while now. I tried to call an hour ago. Didn't you hear your phone ring?"

"Not until just now," Maggie said, trying to come up out of the sleep that still clung to her.

"You should call the doctor again, Sahale," his grandfather said with concern.

"I would have to agree," Bev said, crossing to the side of the bed. Reaching down, she gently pushed the hair off of Maggie's face.

"No, I'm fine, really. I just needed some rest," Maggie tried to protest.

"Let's leave them," Collin began, trying to usher everyone out of the room. "I'll go get hold of the doctor. Ben, will Troy know who to contact?"

Ben met her brother's eyes with a smile. "Yes, he knows how to get hold of Doc McGee."

Collin met Maggie's glance and blew her a kiss, before following everyone else out of the room.

"When did the kids get here?"

Ben sat down next to her and pulled her into his arms. "About an hour ago. Word has spread about your find, Ahawi. The whole town is talking. The kids are sad they weren't there last night. I called Ray and had him send up a crew to rope everything off. It will be waiting for us tomorrow."

Maggie sat up. "No, it will be waiting for us tonight. I'm not wasting any more time."

He took her by the shoulders gently and met her green eyes. "That cave has been undisturbed for centuries, Ahawi. One more day is not going to make a difference. No one is going to get in there before you do. Ray promised that. Right now, I am only concerned about you. It's not good to sleep so much with a head injury. Let's see what the doctor has to say. What's the harm in that?"

Maggie fought the urge to reach out and touch his lips with her fingertips. They looked so soft, almost like velvet. A flash of that morning crept into her mind and she felt her cheeks flush.

"Hey," he said softly as his hand reached out and touched her forehead. He was checking for signs of fever. "You're flushed. Are you all right?"

She suppressed a smile, meeting his warm brown eyes. "I'm fine. Really. I was just thinking about this morning."

"Really?" Ben asked, leaning down to her lips. He kissed her briefly. "I've been thinking of it all day."

Maggie sat up and tried to pull away from his grasp a little. "Ben, I have to..."

Her words were cut short by his lips again. This time he was more insistent and probed at her mouth with his tongue. She did not fight it. Her lips parted and she let him explore her. He tasted sweet, like strawberries and before she knew it, she had threaded her hands gently through his raven hair. As she thought, it was the softest thing she had ever felt. Reason needed to get the better of her, and it needed to do it now. Maggie pulled away quickly and held his gaze.

"Ben, I have to say something."

Dipping his lips to hers again, he brushed them softly.

Maggie closed her eyes and tried to keep a hold on her faculties. "I was talking with Collin this morning..."

"So was I," he said with a grin.

She reached down and took his hands, holding them both tightly. "As hard as I've tried, I can't stop this..."

"Stop what?" He looked at her, puzzled.

"This thing...between us. I've tried. You irritate me so much and I swear that I don't like you..."

Again, his lips met hers. "You do like me." His warm words caressed her skin and she felt her breath catch deep inside of her.

"I do." Feeling a swell of emotion, she pulled back from his grasp. "I do."

Ben reached up and met a tear that fell down her cheek. "And this makes you unhappy?" he questioned, a little afraid of what she might say. Putting himself out there was not something that he had done very often. There was just something about Maggie that made him want more. The thought that she would tell him that she did not feel the same made him anxious.

Maggie looked down, trying to hide her tears from him, trying to formulate her thoughts. "Until today, I never thought it possible to find love with anyone else. Michael has been my constant for so long."

Ben turned and reached for the photo that sat on the bedside table. He looked down at the faces of her three brothers and the one man who had held her heart for so long. There was a lot of love there. He could somehow sense the passion they had for one another. The passion they had for their work.

Maggie reached out for his hand again, pulling his gaze back to hers. "I'm afraid of what I feel for you. Afraid it's too soon."

"It's a new feeling, Ahawi. It's natural to be afraid," he said, trying to comfort her.

"If I give into this, then what does that say about Michael? I will always love him, Ben. I could never forget..."

"I'm not asking you to forget, darlin'. Michael was a part of your life. Knowing him makes you the person you are today. The person that I think I'm falling in love with. I would never ask you to forget those feelings. Trust me when I say that there is room enough in my heart for you and Michael. You do not have to stop loving him to love me."

Maggie met his eyes with tears and a sweet smile. "You would do that?"

"I will. Just promise me that you'll give 'us' a chance. You've come into my life and I don't want to go back to one without you in it. I can take care of you if you'll only let me."

Maggie leaned in and put her arms around him tightly. Again, the feeling of home came to her. It was as if she had spent her whole life with his body pressed against hers. How had this managed to happen in such a short amount of time? Her mind was reeling with it all. Again, as if sensing her thoughts, he pulled her closer. "Sometimes the spirits bring things to us when we least expect it, Ahawi. Those things tend to be what we need most. You are standing at a crossroad now. There are two paths you can take. Only you know which one to go down. I can only hope that I am on the path you choose."

"You've been on that path since I got here," she whispered.

"And your brother? What does he say?"

Maggie felt herself giggle. "He wants me to be happy. He thinks I can find it with you."

Ben pulled back and met her green eyes again. "Well then, I would say that your brother is very wise. I'll not push you, Maggie. I'll be waiting and you will know when your heart is ready. We can take things as slow as you want to. I'm in no hurry."

"Promise me." Maggie searched his eyes and found the truth that she sought. He would wait for her forever if she asked him to.

Leaning in, Ben kissed her deeply and that was all the answer she needed for the moment. Life had come in and pulled the rug out from under her again, and this time she felt it would be okay, as long as his arms were there to catch her. Now, if her head would just stop hurting, that would be something.

Her phone buzzed again, and Maggie sighed with frustration. "There are times when one can be too popular," she said, pulling away from Ben's grasp. Ben smiled at her. "Still, it's nice to know you're loved." The constant hum rose up from the floor and Ben reached down to retrieve the phone, handing it to her. Maggie flipped it open and put it to her ear with another heavy sigh.

"Hello."

"Mags, it's Trevor."

A smile came to her lips and she leaned back against Ben's chest. "Trev, how are ya?"

"I'm good. I think the real question is how are .you? Charlie just sent me a satellite message. Said you fell on a dig. Are you all right, lass?" The concern was heavy in her brother's voice and it left Maggie to wonder if anything could happen to one of them without the other one knowing. She also wondered if Collin had been the one to call Charlie and if he had been told everything.

"I'm fine, Trev. Collin is here with me and my whole crew just went to fetch the doctor again. I'm sure he'll give me a clean bill of health. How goes the dig? Are you finding anything?"

"Nah, not much yet. We've been hampered by rains the past few days, but I'm not ready to throw in the towel just yet. Something will turn up. I heard Ma' went to join Da'."

"Tomorrow, I think she said. She called me this morning. It will be good for them to spend some time together without us kids. Did Charlie say how he was?" Maggie leaned back further into Ben and he wrapped his arms around her tightly.

"He's fine. Up to his knees in dirt, you know. Listen, Charlie also said something about a new fellow. Said Collin liked him. Any truth to that?"

Maggie could hear the smile on her brother's face. "There's some truth to that, Trev. Taking things slow is all, and now we're dealing with this find here. Bev is here with Collin."

Trevor chuckled on the other end. "Coy as ever, Sis. I know I don't need to tell ya, but I will anyway. It's time, Maggie. It's time for you to be happy again. You were never meant to be alone. If Collin is fond of him, then I'm sure that Charlie and I will be too."

Maggie felt a twinge of emotion well up inside her. She had

grown up in the most loving family she had ever seen and the proof was in the support her whole family gave in times of need. In fact it had been Trevor who had flown to Mexico after Michael died to bring her home. They could always count on each other and she had grown to rely on that fact. "Thank you, baby Brother. It means a lot to me. Promise me you'll stay safe. I heard that there were some riots in Costa Rica this past week."

"Aye love, but all is well. You know me, always the cautious one. Take care of yerself, and drop us a line once in a while. Charlie and I miss ya."

"I promise, Trev. Love you."

"Love you most." Maggie snapped her phone shut and looked up into Ben's brown eyes. He gently ran his hand through her auburn locks, smoothing them back.

"Another brother?"

Maggie smiled. "Yes, my youngest. Word travels fast in my family. The Macleod network is a strong one, especially when injury is involved. They've all been so worried about me anyway."

"And did the network spread the news about us?" Ben asked, his eyebrows raised.

"Of course it did."

"Does that bother you?"

Maggie thought about it for a moment. "No, I'm glad, and not that I need it, but they're all happy for me anyway. I'm not sure what you did, but Collin is quite fond of you already."

Ben smiled and leaned down to kiss her again. "I'm glad, Ahawi, because with you is where I want to be."

His lips met hers again and he pulled her closer. Surprised at the lack of reluctance, he ran his hands down her body. Her skin, soft and warm, felt so good to his touch. Ben could not believe that he was actually touching her like this. Things were just starting to get interesting when the knock came. They both jolted up and Ben went to get the door, a bit flustered.

Maggie brought her hand to her face, trying to calm herself. Even without a mirror she knew that she was seven shades of red. As promised, Collin had returned with the doctor. Now, if she could just get a clean bill of health, they could get back out to the cave. That was a possibility that filled her with excitement, but the possibility that Ben would stay with her again tonight filled her with more. She smiled as the thought came to her and she sat up to meet the doctor and her loving brother. What a day this had turned out to be.

Chapter 17

Maggie lay perfectly still, listening to the hum of the machine that was moving inches from her head. Against her better judgment, she had agreed to come to the hospital and get a CT scan. Doc McGee was somewhat concerned that she had a bleed on her brain and would not clear her to go out to the site until she had a scan done. Arguments of protest fell on deaf ears as both Collin and Ben ushered her out of her room and to the emergency room. There was no getting to the site tonight, that was for sure, and the thought filled her with frustration. Maggie did not like wasting time, and this, in her mind, was a definite waste of time.

The machine came to a sudden stop and the florescent lights came back on in the room. Sitting up slightly, she looked around for someone she recognized. A nurse stepped out from the control room and met her with a welcoming smile. Her brightly colored scrubs offended Maggie's senses. *What is it with all the loud colors in this neck of the woods?*

"All done, Ms. Macleod. We will just send the film upstairs so Doc McGee can read it. It shouldn't be too much longer."

"Can you tell me if you saw anything on the film?" Maggie questioned.

"No, I'm afraid I can't say. Don't worry, though, you are in very good hands here." The nurse helped Maggie up off of the table and ushered her out of the imaging room.

Both Ben and Collin were waiting in her curtained-off cubical and smiled on her return.

"Well?" Collin asked, helping her sit down.

Rolling her eyes, Maggie let out a sigh. "We're to wait for the doctor to read the film. Seems that they can't tell me anything."

"It won't be long," the nurse replied, checking Maggie's vitals before leaving them alone.

In an effort to shield her eyes from the harsh fluorescents, Maggie put her hands over her face. "It's too bright in here. Why is it so damn bright?"

Ben reached over and flipped the light switch down. The harsh light was gone, replaced by the soft glow of a light bolted under the counter. "Is that better?" he questioned with concern.

"Yes, thank you." She dropped her hands and looked at both of them. "What will they do if they find a bleed?"

"They will move you upstairs, most likely," Collin said softly.

"I do na' have time for this!"

"You do have time for this, Ahawi. Now sit still and be quiet! They said it won't be long," Ben snapped.

Maggie felt her anger begin to bubble up. She was cranky, tired, a little scared even, and it was causing her to lose control of her temper. Being told what to do was not on a list of things she could tolerate right now. "Ya' know, just because I let you kiss me does na' mean you can talk to me any way ya' please!"

A laugh escaped Ben and he met her eyes with anger of his own. "I'm sure you're right, Maggie. You are always right, aren't you? You know you should be careful. With an attitude like this, someone is bound to take you over their knee. It's a shame I won't be the one to do it." He paused and turned to Collin. "I'll see you back at the Inn. Good luck with her, you're gonna need it." With that, Ben turned, storming out of the cubicle without as much as a glance backward.

"Smooth, Sister of mine. Very smooth," Collin said with a shake of his head.

"Collin, I am in no mood."

"I can see that. You know it won't work."

"I don't know what you're talking about."

"Oh, I think ya' do. Pushing him away will not stop what ya' feel for him. He is genuinely concerned for yer wellbeing, Mags, and he's right, yer attitude leaves a lot to be desired. What the hell is wrong with ya'? Yer acting like a spoiled brat!" Collin's accent floated on the air between them.

Maggie felt stung. As usual, her older brother was right. She knew she was acting like a brat, and what was worse was she didn't know why. Stumbling onto the cave had been big, but she had discovered bigger things before. As hard as she tried, she could not stop this drive within her to keep burying herself in her work. She knew why she was doing that. Again, Collin was right. Pushing Ben away was not going to change what she had begun to feel for him. It would not change anything at all.

Lying back on the exam table, she pulled her legs up to her chest. The back of her hospital gown fell open, but she didn't care. Collin had seen underwear before. "I'm scared, Col," she whispered.

Instinctively, he came to her side, placing his hand on her shoulder. "It's all right to be frightened, love, but I'm sure the Doc will give you a clean bill of health."

"It's not that. I've been hurt before. I'm scared of what I feel, Col. If I give myself to him... If I open my heart up again and something happens... It will kill me this time. I do na' think I can go through that again."

"So you'll do what? Run away from everything good in yer life? That's no way to live, Mags," Collin tried to soothe.

"When I lost Michael, I died myself, Collin. I never want to feel that again." Large, warm tears had welled up in her eyes.

"But loving Michael makes you the person you are today and I have to tell ya, I love the Maggie I know. Do na' be afraid of this. Yer gettin' a second chance, Mags. Do na' throw that away."

"He drives me crazy!" Squeezing her eyes shut, she let those large tears escape her long lashes.

"I can see that. You seem to do the same to him. From what I understand, that's the beginning of a fantastic relationship."

Maggie looked up and met her brother's green eyes. "Ya' think so?"

"I do, Mags. Listen to me and don't run away from this just because Ben challenges you, just because you're afraid."

The nurse came back in, halting their conversation. "All clear, Ms. Macleod. There was no bleed. Doc McGee says you can go to the site tomorrow, but you're not to spend all day there. You're not allowed to drive, either. Is there someone who can help you get around?" she questioned, handing Maggie a form to sign.

"I'll make sure she doesn't drive," Collin said.

Maggie signed the forms and the nurse left them alone again.

"Get dressed. I'll go get the car and meet you out front."

Maggie nodded her head in agreement and watched him leave before she got dressed. Sitting down to slip her shoes on, she wondered how she was going to apologize to Ben. Would he understand her behavior or would he just wash his hands of her and move on? Taking a deep breath, she pulled herself up and began her way down the brightly lit hallway. Dinner was calling and her crew was waiting.

She only hoped Ben would be too.

Chapter 18

*D*inner was already on the table when they arrived back at the Inn. To her surprise everyone was gathered around the largest dining table in the restaurant, including Troy. Everyone that is, except Ben and his grandfather. Maggie felt her heart sink, taking her place next to Bev.

The evening had given way to cooler temperatures and less humidity. A cool night breeze floated in through the open front windows, bringing with it the smell of dogwoods. Troy had dimmed the lights in the dining room for Maggie and the soft glow made the scene seem almost surreal. It was almost right out of the pages of a novel. Small town, beautiful night, new friends, and family gathered around a large dinner table. Maggie should have been happy. She should have felt some sense of peace and belonging, but all she felt was guilt; and what was worse was the laughter coming from everyone. How could they all be so happy when she was so miserable?

After picking at her food for almost an hour, Maggie decided it was time to call it a night. Excusing herself from the table, she made the trudge up the stairs to her room. Closing the door behind her, she heaved a heavy sigh. "Well, you've really done it now, Maggie," she said to herself. Not content to go to bed just yet, she decided that a nice hot bath would do her some good. She started the water, cursing when the water took forever to get hot, and filled the tub. Stripping down, she threw her clothes into the corner before securing her auburn locks high on her head. With the mirror completely covered in steam and the tub full, she turned the water off and slid down into the tub slowly. Beads of sweat formed on her brow within seconds and her skin turned a nice rosy shade. Maggie had just closed her eyes and given herself to relaxation when she heard a knock at her door.

It came again, this time much louder. "Just a minute!" she shouted, pulling herself from the water. Reaching for a large, white towel, she wrapped it around herself and went to the door. She pulled it open. "I'm fine, Collin..." She stopped herself in mid-sentence.

Ben met her gaze and fought the urge to gasp. There she stood in nothing but a towel. Wet with the heat of the water. Her green eyes seemed a much deeper shade and her hair twice as red. He was sure at that moment that he had never seen anything as beautiful as she was, nor would he ever. She was simply stunning and he fought to control himself.

"I just wanted to check on you. Collin said they gave you the okay."

Maggie reached up and took the tie out of her hair, trying to smooth her curls down. "Yes, they said I could go out to the site tomorrow, I just can't drive. I'm sorry, I must look a mess," she said, turning to head back into the room. "Just let me change."

Ben reached out and caught her wrist in his hand, turning her back towards him. Taking her other wrist, he met her glance. "You look beautiful."

Maggie felt the breath catch in her chest. His gaze was almost unnerving. Wanting to look away, she found she could not. "I...I was just taking a bath." Her voice came out softly and she was not sure he had heard her.

"I should leave you, then. Let you get some rest." He leaned in and kissed her forehead.

Maggie felt alarmed. He just got there; she didn't want him to go yet. She wanted him to come in, to stay with her. Quickly, she wrapped her arms around him tightly. "Please stay," she whispered.

"You need rest."

"I need you," she pleaded. He returned her embrace and stepped into the room, shutting the door behind him. "I'm so sorry, Ben. I never meant to make ya' angry with me." She pulled away and met his brown eyes with much emotion. "I'm stubborn, I know. Collin was right, I was acting like a spoiled brat..."

Touching his fingers to her lips, he halted her protests. "I'm sorry I left you there. I guess I was being a brat, too. You drive me crazy, Maggie, I won't lie."

Maggie felt a smile come to her ruby lips. "You drive me mad as well. What do we do about that?"

"Enjoy the ride," he whispered, leaning in and meeting her lips. He kissed her deeply, pressing her to him.

Maggie lost her grip on her towel and it fell around her feet in a pool of heavy white cotton. There she stood before him, her body bare. Ben didn't know if he could control himself.

"Maggie, I don't want to push you..." he paused, licking his lips that had suddenly gone dry, "but seeing you this way, I...I'm not sure I can behave myself. Maybe I should go..."

Maggie took his hand gently in hers and pulled him closer to her. She unbuttoned his shirt with nimble fingers. Reaching the last button, she pulled both sides of the shirt apart and ran her hands down his tan, well-muscled chest. His skin was soft and warm and she felt a shock go through her.

Reaching for her hands, he held them tightly in his. "Ahawi, listen to me. I don't want to rush you..."

"Ben, yer na' rushing me. I know what I'm doing. Please, do na' make me beg..." Her accent hung in the space between them.

Ben smiled at the sound. Even the sound of her voice was beautiful. Maggie filled every sense he had, making him want more. "You will never have to beg for anything," he whispered, bringing his lips to hers again. "All I have is yours." In one motion, he picked her up and held her tightly to his chest, moving towards the big sleigh bed. Laying her on it gently, he stood again, taking in the sight of her. Auburn hair spilled across the white of the sheets and her green eyes were piercing his. Her skin, gently kissed by the sun and dotted with freckles, offered contrast with the paleness of the soft bedding. Kicking his shoes off, he stood frozen, not knowing where to touch her first. He felt his breath quicken and overwhelming need stirred within him. "I have never seen anyone as beautiful as you, Maggie." His voice sounded hoarse.

Maggie took his hand again, lacing her fingers with his. "Come to me."

Slipping his work shirt off, he threw it across the room and lowered himself to her gently. His possessive gaze caressed her entire being, seizing every square inch of her skin as their lips met again. Maggie parted hers and welcomed him in to her mouth. Their tongues explored the recesses of each other's mouths softly, almost patiently. The sensation sent shivers down her spine.

Reaching up, Maggie gently took the tie from Ben's hair. A raven sheet fell across his back and shoulders, tickling the tops of her fingers with its softness. She could feel his need straining through the fabric of his jeans. His body was more than ready for this moment.

Maggie slid her hands between the two of them, enjoying the feel of his skin on hers. Finding the button of his jeans, she un-looped it and pulled the zipper down. Ben took her face in his hands and kissed her softly.

"There is no going back for me after this, darlin'. Are you sure this is what you want?" His brown eyes pleaded with urgency. His need for reassurance seemed great.

Smiling, Maggie ran a hand gently down the curve of his cheek. "I want this, Ben. I want you," she whispered. "From the moment we met, I..." Maggie struggled to find the right words.

Ben leaned down and brushed her nose with his. "I've felt it too."

Wrapping her arms around him, she ran her hands down his chiseled back and over his backside. "You feel so good," she whispered, her eyes closed.

Ben kissed her again, struggling to free himself from his jeans. Kicking them to the bottom of the bed, he finally brought his hands to her waist. Her alabaster skin was warm and smooth under his grasp. As soft as velvet, he thought. His tongue gently traced a line over her lips and moved down the slope of her neck. Maggie closed her eyes and arched into his touch. She could have never known how magical the feel of his hands would be. Her body rose and fell with every breath he took; each trace of his lips. Strong hands rose up her body to her breasts, squeezing them gently.

"Oh," the cry escaped her lips as Ben placed a nipple

between his fingers. He slid the top of his thumb over it ever so slowly and pleasure rose up through her. Pleasure she hadn't felt in a very long time. "Are you really here?" she questioned.

Ben moved up her body again and met her green eyes with his. She found only tenderness in them. Then he blinked and the tenderness was replaced by desire. Maggie thought for a moment she could see a hint of flame in the gold flecks that were scattered through the brown of his irises.

"I'm here, Maggie." His lips met hers softly.

Maggie arched her body against his. Her need had her on the verge of crying out. Feeling that she could take no more, she pushed him over on his back and straddled his waist. Strong hands met her hips and held her in place.

"Easy Maggie..." His voice was raw with need. "I want you so bad, I may not last."

Leaning down, Maggie ran her tongue down his chest. Ben closed his eyes and enjoyed the sensation her hair made as it followed her down the length of his body. She pulled his boxer briefs down, and let him spill into her warm, waiting hands.

"Maggie!" he cried and threw his head back, loving the sensation of her touch. The thought of being inside of her filled all his senses at once. Warm breath caressed his skin and the feeling of overwhelming pleasure taking over.

Maggie brought her lips to the length of him, encompassing his very essence. He tasted sweet and she relished the feel of him in her mouth. Her tongue made short, circular strokes around him and she felt him shudder with pleasure. His fingers gently threaded through her auburn hair in an effort to pull her closer. Maggie took a deep breath to relax her mouth, taking more of him deep inside.

"Maggie...stop..." His voice rough.

Slowly, Maggie raised her head and their eyes met. Her face was flushed with desire and she licked her lips in a teasing gesture. Not being able to take any more, Ben placed his hands under her backside, raising her slightly. She grabbed hold of his strong thighs in an effort to steady herself. Slowly, he lowered her until he felt her velvet softness slide over him, taking every inch.

Maggie threw her head back and arched her back, sitting motionless for a moment. Waves of pleasure rushed over her and she couldn't help but cry out. "Oh, Ben!"

He sat up, shoulders meeting hers. "I'm here, Maggie." Dipping his lips to her, he thrusted slowly. Maggie ground her hips, forging a rhythm with him. He pulled her shoulders back, placing soft kisses over her breastbone.

"That's it, Maggie... Don't stop." Ben's whisper was warm against her ear. His thrusts grew stronger, relishing the feel of her body. She felt as if he wanted to possess it forever and in that moment, that's all she wanted, too.

Maggie tried to slow her pleasure, tried to catch her breath, but it was no use. She hadn't felt this good in so long that her body could wait no longer. Closing her eyes, she threw her head back as her whole body was rocked with ecstasy. Her breath quickened and she cried out, "Ben, yes!"

Taking cues from her, Ben quickened his pace until he could control it no longer. Pleasure shot through his body as Maggie met his lips with hers. She kissed him deeply as he cried out. Almost instinctively, he pulled her as close as he could and held her tightly.

They sat in the middle of the big sleigh bed, bodies intertwined, heaving for air. Maggie had wrapped her arms and legs around him, wanting to be as close to him as she could. As before, the feeling of home washed over her. More important to her, though, was the fact that she felt safe. It had been too long since she had felt that. In his arms was the only place she wanted to be, of that she was sure.

Ben pulled her down to the pillows with him, never once losing his grip on her body. "Thank you, Maggie," he whispered.

Maggie giggled. "No, thank you." She reached for his hand and their fingers interlaced. "I'm glad you came back."

"I had to," he said, kissing her hair, "I left my bag here."

Maggie giggled again. "Are you going to stick with that story?"

"For now."

Sated and perfectly content, Maggie closed her eyes. She knew that the depths of sleep were not far behind.

Ben kissed her hair again. "I've got you. Rest well."

"Ben, you won't leave me?" she asked, sliding her leg across his body in an effort to get closer to him. "Shh. I'll be here when you wake. I will be here as long as you want me to be."

"And if I always want you?" she questioned, traces of sleep lacing her voice.

"Then you will always find me here. Now rest, darlin'. We have a big day tomorrow." Ben stroked her hair and listened as her breathing grew deeper. Pulling her closer, he allowed his eyes to close, letting the depths of deep sleep claim him. For now, on this beautiful night, all was right in his world.

Chapter 19

The morning had come too early for Maggie and Ben. They were having a tough time tearing themselves away from each other's bodies. Every time she tried to get out of bed, he would pull her back in and kiss her until she was breathless. Laying there, intertwined with his body and the cool cotton sheets, Maggie was sure she had felt what heaven was like. Things were just getting interesting again when her phone rang. It was Collin wondering why they weren't downstairs for breakfast. Maggie assured him that they would be down right away and they both got up to get ready for the day. Once down there, she found herself reassuring everyone that she was okay and up for the trek to the cave. With Ben's assurance of her health, everyone agreed and they all piled into their cars to make the trip out to the site.

Ben, Bev, Maggie, and Collin stepped out of the Suburban and grabbed backpacks as Ally, Rick, and Ellen approached. Ben spoke with his back to the girls. "Where did you get the chicken?"

"Oh, what's he talking about?" Ellen asked with a giggle.

"What chicken?" Ally asked. Ben then turned and looked at Rick blankly.

"Oh, I'm sorry. I thought Rick was riding on a chicken but I guess he's just wearing shorts."

"Smart ass!" Rick said, shoving Ben. "I don't see you wearing shorts."

"Someone has to break a trail through the briars," Ben

replied.

"Are you sure you're up to this hike, Maggie?" Ally asked, picking up Maggie's backpack.

"Try and stop me. No, you're not taking that for me, girlie. I can manage, thanks," Maggie laughed in an attempt to seem more energetic than she felt at the moment.

"How far are we from the cave?" Bev inquired.

"Only about half a mile," Ben answered, "but it's mostly uphill. We'll take as many breaks as we need. Not all of us have poultry to ride."

"This is the last freakin' time I am wearing shorts, I swear to god!" Rick commented, walking toward the hillside with Ellen poking his shoulder.

"Do you shave them or wax them?" she laughed.

Walking up the hillside, Ben kept as close as he could to Maggie, who seemed to be living off of adrenalin. Collin and Bev appeared to be enjoying the hike, although the pace of their steps was hindered by the terrain somewhat. Looking back to make certain he was a few arms lengths ahead of the rest, Ben drew a machete and cut the underbrush to make the trail more passable. Fifteen minutes and a few hundred yards up the path, he decided it was time to force a break. "Nice view, huh?" he said, looking out across the river below.

"Ma would love this. It's so lush, like Scotland," Collin commented, drinking from his water bottle. "May Apples. I've never seen so many." He took a few steps away from the group for a closer look. Ben turned to notice Maggie had slowly walked several paces ahead of them. She would push herself too hard if they let her, he knew.

"Yeah, they're everywhere this time of year," Ben replied. "Some people even sell them."

"Hey, Ben," Rick called, catching his breath, "wouldn't it be easier to get here from Whiskey Run? I know that Huggins guy with the farm. We could take four-wheelers from his place even."

Ben looked at the rest of the weary group, and commented, "And you never mentioned this before now because...?"

"Because he likes seeing me get eaten by bugs!" Ellen exclaimed, scratching her legs.

"Can you look into that, Rick?" Maggie hollered back,

now almost twenty yards ahead of them. Collin rolled his eyes and quickened his pace to catch her. Ben, and then the others, followed him. Bev stopped from time to time to grab a few pictures, asking Ally and Rick questions about the area. The rugged climb appeared to get easier, at least for Maggie, who was pulling them along at a steady pace. She was the first to pop over the hill and reach their tents. She found them as they left them the night she fell, but continued on and passed them up as if without notice.

"Ahawi, slow down! You're killing us here!" Ben called to her. He caught up to her and reached out to touch her shoulder.

"Where's the tree? Where's the tree?" Maggie questioned with glee. Her excitement was hard to miss. She spotted it quickly before walking over to it. Reason appeared to get the best of her. She turned to wait for the others. Her eyes gleamed with excitement, smiling back at them. "Okay, everyone. Are you ready to be amazed? Sahale, what are you waiting for?"

Ben rolled his eyes and smiled back at her. "All right, I'm getting to it darlin'." Ben winked at her before he pulled the tree from the opening. Rick and Ally went to the other side to lend a hand.

"Now wait, let's be safe," Bev said, halting everyone. She pulled a gas detector from her pack. "This goes in before anyone, and I do mean anyone," she said, looking at Maggie. She approached the opening and shined her flashlight down it. Maggie also took her light out and crowded around with everyone else.

"Here, Bev. I'll go first," Ben said, grabbing the rope, still attached to the nearby tree. He reached out for the detector before getting down on his knees to descend. "Hey, Maggie, is this about where you landed on your ass?"

"Oh, just go!" Maggie laughed, enjoying the playful banter.

Ben had no trouble keeping his footing with the help of the rope. As soon as his feet were on level ground he looked at the detector.

"It will beep if there's CO, Ben," Bev hollered down to him.

Ben read the screen and yelled, "Nothing. No CO!"

Maggie was already ahead of the others and Ben watched her descend protectively. As soon as she reached the floor of the cave, Collin followed. When he was inside, he took the gas detector from Ben and walked around the perimeter of the room, just to be safe.

"Ohhh..." The excitement was evident in Maggie's voice. She was not often heard to squeal in delight, but she found that she couldn't help it here. Walking over, she stood by the original steps leading down to the room. "This is Cherokee, isn't it?"

Ben walked over to her side. "Yep."

"What does it say?"

Ben studied it for a few seconds, his forehead wrinkling a bit. "Live bands every Friday and Saturday night."

Maggie squeezed his arm gently, laughing. "Come on!"

"Well, I have no clue. This is older than other cave writings I've seen. It might even be an older dialect of the Cherokee language. We'll have to get my grandfather to read it."

"That's unusual. I thought you said you thought this was Adena?" Bev questioned, surveying the room.

"Well, based on the dating I think we'll find here, it is... Don't you think?"

Bev didn't answer but continued to examine the floor and its crystal mosaic. "Let's have a meeting." The others closed in and listened intently. "There are several possibilities here and it's obvious that this is an extremely valuable discovery. So, I think that we're going to be extremely diligent here. We might even have to call some others in after our initial inspection today. Rick, Ally, Ellen, I want you to start on the walls. If you find anything, brush off the dust, but carefully. We don't want to all smother until we can get some fresh air flowing through here. We also don't want anything to chip off the walls. They are extremely old, as you can clearly see. I want you all to avoid walking on the mosaic as well. Maggie, let's you and I get to work and clean this off." With that Maggie and Bev gently dusted off the beautiful floor in the center of the room.

"What can I do, Bev?" Ben questioned.

"Watch for bears, I suppose," Bev said with a little giggle. "I'm joking. Take some pictures of that writing. The steps, too. As a matter of fact, take pictures of everything. Then see if you can figure out how those steps exited this space. We know whoever used this cave didn't slide down on their butts like some other people we know."

"Did you notice? The echo, or lack of an echo in here?"

Maggie asked, winking at Bev. Bev held still for a moment and listened to the other's voices. "Now that you mention it, yes. How odd," she said with a puzzled look.

"Bev, like the Aztecs and Incas, the Adena were mathematically advanced. That has most certainly played into the creation of this space."

"That's a good point, Maggie. That's a very good point. This room seems perfectly round, too. Obviously that's by design as well. The question we have to answer here is why." Bev looked at Maggie, taking in her smile of excitement. "You were right, Maggs. This is big." She rose to her feet and shined her light to the ceiling of the room. "Very big indeed."

The light revealed a few bats, and some more drawings.

"See?" Maggie replied, looking upwards. "All these drawings, they've been covered in places by mineral deposits from water seeping down. That takes hundreds of years for formations that thick."

"You managed to absorb a lot of details in a matter of minutes, and with a concussion to boot."

"I tried to remember everything I saw," Maggie said with a look of reflection, "but...it's funny really. I swear that I worked on this in my dreams last night. I could recall every detail."

"Ewwww!" Ellen screamed at some bats flying by, disturbed by the intrusion.

"They're just common brown bats," Collin responded. "They're harmless."

"They're rats with wings, and I hate 'em!" Ellen squealed, looking around for more. "I have the worst headache! Does anyone have anything?"

"I got some ibuprofen," Rick said, sitting down beside Ellen on the large stone shelf and looking in his backpack.

"Okay, I found the closure rock," Ben said, catching his breath. "It's pretty big, but I'll bet we could chain it to my four-wheeler..."

"We might want to do that later, but for now let's not disturb any more than we need to..." Bev became distracted by a glimmer of light that seemed to be coming from a foot beyond Ally's progress on the walls of the cave. "Ally," she said, shining her light on the wall, "please clean a spot off there." Ally stepped a few feet to her left, just to the right of the steps and brushed dust and debris out of the way Bev's light drew no reflection while Ally worked, but once done, she stepped aside and pointed. Bev immediately pointed her light as per Ally's directions and the room lit up as if someone had turned on a disco light. White sparkling light spots fell everywhere, the majority of them mainly on the large stone shelf across the room where Rick and Ellen sat.

"What in the world?" Maggie questioned, following Bev in and touching the shiny surface.

"It appears to be very smooth, probably mica, but what impresses me is the precision," Bev said. She and Ally continued wiping away the dust with care.

"There's some over here also," Maggie commented, running her brush gently along the wall a few feet away. In time the three met up, their paths connecting. They realized instantly that the wall was one large, smooth reflective surface. "Incredible. Absolutely incredible. Look at the uniform shape. Have you ever seen anything like this on such a scale?"

"I've honestly got nothing to compare it to," Bev replied, stepping back for a better look.

"Would y'all excuse me?" Ellen asked, getting up on wobbly legs. "I just need to go up for some fresh air."

"Go up there with her, please, Rick," Maggie replied.

The two scaled the incline aided by a rope as the others continued their work. Collin took pictures as they made progress through the cave. Ben and Ally hunted along the perimeter of the room for any other anomalies they could find. "Ahawi, take a look at this," Ben called to her from the north wall of the cave. There, the perfect curvature gave way to a recessed area filled in with clay and rocks. It seemed to be some sort of large passageway.

"This room might be the tip of the iceberg it seems," said Bev, approaching them. "This could very well lead to other rooms."

"I don't think so," Ben answered, reading the compass on his watch. "This wall has to be very close to the cliffs, maybe just a few yards away. That's North," he said, pointing to the opening.

Bev looked around. "This room is about fifty or sixty feet in diameter. Ben..."

"I'm on it," Ben said, hurrying past them and out of the cave. Making his way out of the opening, he saw Ellen and Rick standing at the edge of the cliff, looking out over the river. Ellen was laughing as they threw rocks down the hill. "Rick, what do you think it is from me to you, a sand wedge?" Ben hollered.

Rick studied and replied, "Nah, not even a lob wedge." With that he stepped off the distance, walking toward Ben and counting. "Thirty-five yards. Maybe a sand wedge for you."

Ben smiled. "If there wasn't a lady present I'd tell you what you could do with that wedge. How are you feeling, Ellen?"

"I feel fine now. Just needed some air. I'll be there in a few minutes."

"Okay, take as long as you need. Rick, can you cut me a pole, maybe six or eight feet?" Ben asked, tossing his encased knife at him.

"Sure."

"Oh, and, guys," Ben said in a lower voice, "keep the beer out of sight."

"Yeah," Rick said with a grin. Ellen turned red with embarrassment. Ben hurried back down to the cave with Ellen close behind. He entered the room and counted his paces until he reached the north wall. "Bev, near as I can figure, we are only a few yards from the face of the cliff here. Hey! What did you find?"

In her hands, Maggie held a clay pot, which appeared to be intact, "There's so many of these in here, Ben!"

Collin touched the pot and commented, "This is sealed, but it might be something that I can have analyzed. I'll make some calls when we get back to the Inn."

"This one is definitely sealed," said Bev, placing the pot down on the floor where she found it. A pile of clay and rocks was on the floor from their efforts and the opening was now taking shape. The walls of this new room were round, smooth, and it was much wider than a doorway.

"Are you taking notes, Maggie?"

"Yes, of course I am," Maggie said, scribbling quickly on her legal pad.

"Good. Then I'll make you a deal. Sit down, take notes, tell us if you start feeling tired or light headed, and you can finish the day with us."

Maggie didn't argue since she felt she was the best one to be taking notes anyway. She sat on the large stone shelf across the room, getting up from time to time to stretch her legs or direct some of the action. They continued to work, only stopping briefly for a short lunch break, and Maggie reveled in the fact that everyone was just as excited as she was about the work they were doing.

Ben, meanwhile, had managed to dig his way through the newly found tunnel until light from the early evening shone through it. He was correct in his earlier thinking. It was a straight shot of about fifteen feet to the face of the sheer sandstone cliff that hung above Route 2, and it was now open again after countless years. He felt a sense of pride for his people in this accomplishment.

By the time evening enveloped them, they had volumes of notes and hundreds of photos to go through. Collin, feeling certain that Maggie was being perky for the benefit of the others, had to question, "How are you doing, Sister of mine?"

It had been a long day for all of them, but especially for her. Maggie looked up at her brother, feeling his concern for her, but in fact she was truthful when she answered them. "Honestly, I'm fine. Really. This has been one of the most exciting days of my life. I'm sure that I will sleep well tonight, though."

"I'm so tired!" Ally commented, walking towards Maggie and sitting down next to her. The excitement of the day had taken its toll on everyone.

"It's almost seven. Perhaps we should tie things up for the day?" Bev asked.

"Fine with me," Collin answered, stretching. "I could use a dip in the hot tub."

"Oh, I'd fall asleep if I did that," Ellen responded. "Maggie, you feeling okay?"

"Yes. If we had dinner here, I could go another shift, but we would need lights. That's something to add to our list of supplies. We do need to get off the hill though. I was thinking we should have a working dinner, maybe at the Inn?"

"My thoughts exactly," Bev answered. "Collin, could you put those pictures on your laptop and bring it to dinner?"

"Yep."

"I've got a copy of the writing from the wall there. I'm sure my grandfather will be able to interpret it," Ben replied, sitting

122

down between Ally and Maggie. He rubbed Maggie's shoulders gently. She leaned into him, feeling the tension leave her at his touch. Magical, she thought.

"Maggie, Ben said we could use his tent tonight. Me, Ellen, and Rick thought it would be fun to stay up here," said Ally.

"Fine with me. You can use my tent, too. Just watch out for BEARS!" she said, gently bumping Ben. "Damn, darlin'! If you want to get physical you only need to ask," Ben whispered in her ear with raised eyebrows.

"Physical will come later if I have my way," Maggie whispered back. With a wink to Ben she got to her feet from the stone, her energy renewed.

Chapter 20

"**W**ell! If you don't look like a new fawn this evening. How's the noggin?" Troy asked Maggie when she came down the steps from the second floor of the Inn. She had dressed casually in shorts and a West Virginia t-shirt that she bought in the gift shop. Her auburn curls were pulled back in a ponytail that swayed from side to side with her steps.

"The noggin is fine, Troy. Thank you for asking. I was wondering, if it won't be an issue, we'd like to have the back dining room for a sort of working dinner tonight. Would that be all right?"

"Not a problem. Do you know about what time?"

"Well..." Maggie began with a sigh, "Collin must have fallen asleep in the hot tub, and Bev and I are trying to reach Ben and John, so I'm guessing...about an hour?"

"Okay, I'll have a table ready by 8:30 then."

"Thanks, Troy," she called, making her way down the hallway to the pool. Just as she thought, her brother was lounging in the hot tub, his head back, sipping a Bud Lite. "No Heineken?"

"You know, little Sister, this is going to be much like a vacation for me."

"Looks like it," Maggie said, taking a seat beside him on a lounge chair. She took the beer from him for a sip. "This is big, Collin. There's no tellin' where this will take us! I have so many questions. It's just wide open."

"You've always made us proud, Mags, but this...well, this is big all right," Collin said, drinking the last drops of beer from the bottle. "I'm starved. Are we going to do dinner soon?"

"Yep, just as soon as we're all ready. I just need to get in touch with Ben and John. He hasn't been answering the phone."

Collin raised his gaze and met his sister with a smile. "You know, I saw the two of you today. Was that a bit of sexy banter I saw between you? Glad you took my advice little Sister and made up with Ben," he teased her.

Maggie giggled before handing the beer back to him. "Cornball! What makes ya' think ya' had anything to do with it?" She winked at him before getting up and heading for the door. "Dinner's at 8:30. Do na' be late," she called to him.

* * *

Ben was telling his grandfather about their day. The old man sat watching TV, making himself at home and having no problem accomplishing this. He nibbled on some peanuts with his shoes off and eyes fixed on the screen.

"So, near the entrance of this cave there's this writing. I think it's Cherokee," Ben said, handing his grandfather a copy of the text.

"Uh huh," John answered, barely taking his eyes off the TV.

"Well, Grandpa, we were wondering if you would tell us what it says. This must be an older dialect...I'm not familiar with it."

John's expression never wavered when he got out of his chair. He held the paper in his hand, walking to the sink and filling a glass of water. He drank it down, and when he was finished, he turned to his grandson, "Is it really important that they know?"

"Yes, it is. We need to learn everything we can about this cave, and this might be the most defining piece of the puzzle that we have."

John sat back down, placing the paper in his lap. "It is the words of our people. The white man has never understood our way. What makes you think they will understand the words when they are made English?"

Ben struggled for a response. Their relationship had always been built on love and respect and he didn't want an argument to create any kind of a wedge between them that he would be sorry for later. He sat down on the couch, looking at the old man. "Can you explain it to me, then?"

John did not look at the paper as he spoke. "Our people cared for the land many years before the white man came. Thousands of years before the Cherokee, our ancestors gave us this gift of taking care of the earth, and we have honored them by doing just that. It is an important thing."

"Yes, Grandpa, I realize that."

"These words say that. They say that our people have promised to keep the cave as it has been for thousands of years. It is a sacred place."

"I see," Ben replied. He knew exactly where this conversation was heading. "Grandpa, I believe what you say. Now please believe me when I tell you that this is an important and...valuable thing that I ask. Could you tell me the exact words so I can write this down?"

"Valuable? The white man has never known what is valuable. They buy and sell land, and even people, as if we are not one with the earth!" John said in a strong voice that alerted Ben to his sensitivity on the subject matter.

"I know, Grandpa, but I also know that they would like to learn about us. Can we help them see our ways? You must have seen in your life that they are not entirely savage or stupid. So let's try to help them see our logic for once. Besides, if we don't save this cave, Ray and his team are going to blast it to hell. We won't be able to do anything to stop them if they don't know about it."

John sat in deep thought for a moment before finally looking at his grandson again. "I will help you help them, but this is more complicated than it might appear, Sahale. First, I want you to tell me what you saw. What did these people find?"

John listened as Ben described the cave, at times nodding his head in understanding. All the while, Ben got the impression that the old man knew much more about the cave than he let on. By the time he had finished describing everything he'd seen, Ben was convinced that this was indeed a very sacred place to his people, without his grandfather uttering a single word.

John then spoke, saying, "I suppose anyone could tell you the meaning of these words so I will do it. I've already missed this 'Munsters.' Gotta get you out of my hair so I can watch the next one." He pointed at the TV.

Ben laughed. "I'm sorry."

"It's the one where Herman takes the family on vacation. Reminds me of the time you and I went fishing in that dead creek and never caught a thing."

"We still had a good time though, Grandpa."

"Yeah, I suppose we did." John smiled at the memory, "Got any more change for the vending machine?"

Ben looked at the stand beside the chair and saw three empty bags and two cans of soda. "We're having dinner downstairs soon," he said, grabbing a pen and notepad. "Now what does this say?"

"Do people smoke there?"

"We'll get a non-smoking table. Can you read that okay?"

"Yes, I can see it fine. What do they have to eat?"

"They have a lot of stuff, Grandpa. You'll love it and I want everyone to meet you."

"They might get a kick out of me, huh? This place you see is sacred to us. Do not enter here with a heart filled with..." He continued as Ben wrote his words verbatim, stopping several times to clarify. It seemed to Ben that his grandfather recalled the words from memory rather than reading them from paper. When they finished, the phone rang.

"Hello?" Ben answered.

"Can you and your grandfather be down for dinner in about thirty minutes?"

"Yes, Maggie. We were just translating this writing. It is Cherokee."

"Oh, excellent! I will see you soon, and hurry...I miss you."

"See you soon. Bye, Ahawi," Ben said, hanging up the phone with a smile. He stood in contemplation. The last few days had been like an exciting ride down a country road in a convertible, and now he had to figure out a way to put the top up, to find shelter from the approaching storm. He knew that Maggie wasn't going to like this.

"Do you see," John said, getting up from his chair, "the secrets of this sacred place have been kept by our people for thousands of years. I know we will not throw this away and dishonor those before us."

"I know, Grandpa, but the fact is...I don't know if we have much of a choice."

"Where is your heart?" John asked. "You must answer this when you pick a path to follow. If you do that, then it will be the right choice."

"Grandpa..." Ben struggled for words. Where was his heart? He was excited at the prospect of helping Maggie with her discovery and more, yet unsettled by the ramifications of doing just that. "Have faith in me. That's all I will ask." He looked to the old mad for a sign of affirmation.

"Why doesn't Grandpa just kick Herman's ass sometimes?" John's attention was once again on the TV screen.

"Uh...I don't know. We're going down to eat in about thirty minutes. Do you need to get ready?"

"No, I'm ready. Lily is hotter than Marilyn, don't you think? I think so."

Chapter 21

*B*en and John walked into the dining room, finding Bev and Maggie looking out the window into the courtyard. "Sahale, what kind of bush is that? The one there with the purple flowers?" Maggie asked, pointing.

"That's a rhododendron," Ben said, approaching the two ladies.

"See! Bev thought it was mountain laurel."

"No, we don't have much mountain laurel around here. They're all rhododendrons," Ben replied, turning to see his grandfather lagging behind, taking his time in joining them.

"How was your day, Mr. Adams?" Bev asked in an effort to involve him in the conversation.

"Not bad. I took a nice walk, then a nap."

"I want to walk around town soon, but this humidity! Is this typical for this time of year?"

"Yeah, pretty much. I could use a beer."

"We'll get one in a minute, Grandpa. Where's Collin?" Ben asked.

"He's either on the phone or he snuck back in that hot tub," Maggie said, looking at her watch. "Maybe I'll call him."

Maggie had just finished dialing when Collin entered the room. He pulled his phone from his pocket, saw it was her, and answered, "Hello, who is this?"

Maggie laughed, closing her phone. "You're late, and we're

starving."

"Sorry, I was just arranging for a GC, IR, and UV on those urns, if that's okay with you?"

"Yes, in fact that's wonderful," Maggie said, taking a seat at the table and the others following suit. As she had requested, the table was roomy enough for the five of them to eat and spread out some work.

Just then a waitress entered the room and took their drink orders. "And we'd also like a bottle of merlot," Maggie said with a big smile. "We're celebrating tonight."

"With good reason," Bev added. "I can't wait to see the pictures, but I know I'll see them and want to go back up that hill tonight."

"Well let's have a look at them, then," Collin said, opening his laptop and turning it on. They all gathered around behind him and watched him scroll through the photos. By the time they were done, drinks had arrived and their food orders had been taken. Everyone sat down again, feeling a heavy sense of excitement. Maggie noticed that Ben seemed more subdued than his usual self and reached for his hand when he sat beside her.

"Hey there. You okay?" she asked, leaning in close to him.

"Yes...yes, I'm fine," Ben replied as if awakened from a trance. "Just tired, that's all," he said, trying to reassure her. Squeezing her hand back, he winked at her. "Must have gotten too much sun today."

"Truth be told, I'm exhausted myself. I promise I'll let you get some sleep tonight." Her voice was soft.

"And maybe I promise to not let you get any..." His words hung in the air between them as Maggie felt herself begin to blush.

During dinner the conversation at times steered more toward the weather, the surroundings of the hotel, and personal anecdotes, yet always found its way back to the cave. When they had finished and were awaiting coffee, Maggie began, "Alright, as far as tomorrow goes, Collin, you're seeing to lab work, Bev and I are heading straight up the hill, and Ben, you're picking up the things on this list at the hardware store, correct?"

"Sounds good to me," Ben replied.

"Can you take me home first, Ben?" John asked.

"Home? Why do you need to go home?" Ben asked with

concern.

"I have to water those tomato plants....and check my messages."

"Grandpa, Uncle Joe is taking care of that. Besides, we need you here. You're going to be a big help."

Maggie looked concerned, but continued. "Ben, you were also going to see about getting access to the area from a farm?"

"Yes, I'll do that. We'll be able to drive up the ridge and have a lot easier walk in. We can even take stuff in on four wheelers"

"Four wheelers," John said under his breath, rolling his eyes.

"Great. It would be nice to get the main entrance to the steps cleared as soon as possible. Bev, can you think of anything else?"

"Not off the top of my head. I'm still reeling, myself. This is very exciting."

Just then the coffee and deserts arrived. Everyone had ordered the apple pie. They couldn't resist it, as the aroma of fresh baking had filled the Inn all evening. "This is so good!" Maggie said, looking at Bev.

"Yes, it certainly is. We should see about getting one to take to the kids for tomorrow."

"Oh, that's right. I forgot they're staying up on the hill tonight. Probably eating hot dogs and s'mores," Maggie laughed, looking at Ben.

"Well, whatever it is, I'm sure it's not this good," Ben added, devouring the pie.

* * *

Up on the hill outside the cave it was a much different scene. The flames of the fire had begun to blow in the wind that had developed, coming off a distant storm. Lightning flashed several miles away, but went largely unnoticed by the three who each had empty beer cans at their feet.

"Oh shit, guys! We need to pick these up before morning," Ally said in an inebriated voice, stumbling out of her chair.

Ellen laughed. "I swear, Ally, you're a teetotaler!" She bent to help her off the ground.

"Let me tell you, I think we need more beer. Rick's going to have to run down and get a case."

"No," Rick said with a laugh. "I'm not going off this hill in the dark. We have...three left." He pulled the three cans out and distributed them, drinking from his can. "Ahh, nectar of the Gods!" Placing his can down next to his chair, he gathered up all the empties, smashing the cans with his foot and stuffing them in a grocery bag.

"Ally, are you okay?" Ellen laughed. The answer was not as important; she just wanted to hear Ally's response.

"Hell yes, what do I look like here?" Ally said, plopping down close to the fire.

"You look like a marshmallow waiting to be s'mored," Rick answered.

"Well, s'more me, baby!" Ally yelled, falling backward on the ground. She grabbed her head when it hit a rock that she hadn't noticed before. "Ouch! Where did that come from?"

"It's been there all evening," Rick said, helping her sit up again. Ellen giggled at the scene. Ally sat with her eyes closed, so Rick thought it best to lower her back gently to lay on the ground again. Walking toward the cliff he looked out at distant lightning. "I hope we don't get rained on."

"You think we'll be alright in the tents?" Ellen asked, sipping her beer.

Rick turned to her. "You guys will. Looking at Sahale's tent, I'd say I'd better hope it passes us."

"I'm not as afraid of the lightning as the prospect of needing more beer." Ellen laughed at her own joke. A little snort escaped her and she laughed even harder.

"I want beer," Ally yelled again.

"I thought she'd passed out," said Rick. "Here, help me get her in the tent." The two each took an arm and helped her into Maggie's tent, took her boots off, and laid her on a sleeping bag.

"Aww, you guys can't leave me!" Ally cried.

"We're not leaving you, sweetie. We're going to be right out here by the fire," Ellen soothed, patting her drunk friend's head.

"Alright, just don't go making a mess out there cause... cause I'd have to clean it up," Ally said with a cough, closing her eyes as Rick and Ellen zipped the door shut.

"You think she'll be alright for tomorrow?"

"Oh yeah," Rick said, rolling his eyes at the thought. "We'll make her drink some water and maybe there's some coffee in the supplies here." The two stood by the fire and watched the flames dance in a gentle breeze. The storm did not seem to be getting any closer, but the air seemed lighter and cooler as if rain was just miles away. Rick grabbed a flashlight and turned it on, testing the battery power. Ellen took a blanket from her backpack and wrapped it over her shoulders.

"I took my flannel shirt off and left it in the cave today," Ellen said. "I wish I hadn't."

"Let's go get it, then," Rick said, walking toward the path to the hole.

"Oh, you're nuts. I don't want to go down there in the dark."

"It's as light now as it was today," Rick replied.

"I know, but we'd have to climb down in there...and I have shorts on."

Rick stopped at the edge of the opening, grabbing the rope. "I think you're chicken. I'm going down in, so you can be a chicken here or inside. Take your pick." He scaled the incline down into the cave. Ellen stood still for a moment, and then decided to join him. When the two reached the main room, Rick shined the light all around. "There's your shirt," he said, walking over to the large rock shelf where she had sat earlier in the day.

Ellen followed, removing the blanket from her shoulders, placing it on the rock, and sat down, putting the flannel shirt over her shoulders. "We should get a good grade for this, huh?" she questioned with a smile.

"We should get famous for this," Rick added. "Imagine the luck. Maggie just falling down this hole the night they spent up here."

"Yeah," Ellen replied. Rick sat down beside her, and flicker of lightning caught their eyes from across the room. It filtered through the passage that Ben had opened completely to the cliff. "At least now that door is open we can have some air moving through here."

"Yeah, more light in here tomorrow, too."

"Maggie seems to be pretty headstrong," Ellen snickered.

"You think they did it?"

"Did what?" Rick chuckled.

"You know! Do you think they had sex when they were all alone up here?" Ellen asked. "I know I would have jumped him."

"Oh, you would?"

"Well, yeah, I mean... Ben's a good looking guy. Don't you think Maggie's attractive?"

Rick thought for a minute. "I don't know...Well...yeah, I mean, you put her in the right clothes, I guess so."

"Oh, come on, Rick! She's beautiful. She just needs to loosen up is all."

"Yeah, that's what I mean," Rick said, shining the light on Ellen. "She has a nice body, and maybe if she wore...something like that." Rick directed the light on the cleavage Ellen was showing from the top of her low-cut tank top. "You know, showed a little cleavage, like you do." With that, Rick placed his fingertips on Ellen's shirt, pulling it out from her chest. "Very nice," he said.

Ellen giggled. "She's a doctor of archeology, you idiot. She doesn't have to show cleavage, but, thank you," she replied.

Rick's fingers continued to probe down the front of her shirt. In the same instance Rick worked up the nerve to place his other hand fully over her breasts. Ellen lunged forward, kissing him hard. They were both surprised. It was not the type of kiss typical of first kisses, but powerful, bordering on violent. One so deep and bold that within seconds they found themselves entwined and tugging at each other's clothes on top of the blanket. It was as if they were seized by some mystery force. Something so strong, pleasure so intense, they had no control over it. Their cries mingled with the sound of the wind whistling down the tunnel to the main room. Neither seemed to care about the hardness of the rock under them, they just thrust against one another uncontrollably.

"Oh god, Rick!" Ellen screamed, her nails digging into his back. Rick didn't answer. They rolled over and Ellen lay on top of him. This force was so powerful and earth shattering that within minutes both reached a climax. They shattered, spiraling down into the depths of an intense pleasure neither had experienced before. Holding each other tightly without breaking their embrace, Ellen tried to pull him closer to her.

"My god that was hot!" Rick whispered, catching his breath.

"Yeah," Ellen said, panting. "Yeah, it was."

The two smiled, and their lips met again. Their passion far from over, they lay exploring one another until the unseen force took hold of them for another time. More than an hour later, Rick and Ellen lay out of breath, attempting to gather strength to move. They had no recollection of the rain that fell, the crashes of lightning, or the wind that had just ceased blowing past their entwined bodies.

"I wonder if Ally's alright up there," Ellen said, breaking the silence.

"Yeah...yeah, I guess we should go check on her," Rick replied. Reluctantly, they got dressed and crawled out of the entrance to the cave. They were met with a thick fog that had rolled in due to all the humidity. "Crap, it rained!"

"It rained a lot. The fire is out. Are you sure you know which way to go?"

"It's right over here," Rick called, pulling her along the trail. When they reached the encampment, they took in the sight of Ben's tent, flat on the ground. The only sounds were the drum beat of water falling off the leaves overhead and Ally's snoring.

"Oh, lord." Ellen giggled, "I have to sleep with that!"

"Looks like I do, too." The two crawled into the tent, squeezing in tight next to Ally.

"I hope it doesn't rain again," Ellen said, closing her eyes.

Rick wrapped his arm around her, laying a kiss on her neck. "We'll be okay if it does." They fell into a deep sleep, never stirring until morning.

Chapter 22

*L*ightning flashed, filling the whole room. Maggie jumped, the thunder shaking the windows of her room. The storm was right over them and the rain fell wildly on the roof. The fresh scent of rain floated in through the open window, bringing with it the smell of the dogwoods that dotted the landscape. Maggie took a deep breath and took the scent in. She was trying to calm herself. The storm seemed fitting for her mood. Something was wrong. She could feel it deep in her bones and it was in Ben's expression all evening. He had been distant, almost troubled, and it bothered her.

Thinking that she had paced the floor of her room enough, she turned and went to the floral sofa. After dinner, everyone had gone their separate ways. Collin had returned to the Jacuzzi and Bev had retired to her room for the evening. John had insisted on going home, so Ben had kissed her, promising that he would be back as soon as he could. Now, here she sat.

Maggie reached up and wrapped an auburn curl around her fingers, a gesture she only did when she was nervous, and that she was. John had seemed irritated throughout dinner. Now she was afraid that she knew why. He didn't like her. He didn't like his grandson getting involved with her. Ben had undoubtedly told his grandfather about their new relationship. Does John dislike the idea so much that he wants to keep us apart? she wondered. The thought didn't sit well with her. Ben had come into her life when she needed him the most. Feelings had begun to develop and she didn't want to let them go. She knew what they were, knew how to define them. Quite simply, Maggie was falling in love with him. The prospect of that both excited and frightened her.

Exhaustion set in. It had been such a long day and she knew that she had pushed herself harder than she should have. Maggie pulled herself up from the sofa and made her way over to the bed. Lightning filled the room again as she lay down, pulling the quilt up tightly around her. The night air was cool for a change and she felt a little chilled in just her chemise. Having given Ben the key to the room, she knew it would be okay to get some rest. Maggie closed her weary eyes, the thunder rolling. Sleep would come, but it would not be peaceful until Ben was next to her.

* * *

"I wish you'd change your mind, Grandpa, and come back to the Inn with me," Ben pleaded. The two men sat on the front porch of John's house, watching the storm that was quickly coming their way. John had been silent the whole drive and it bothered Ben. His grandfather was never at a loss for words.

"I have much to do here, Sahale. Go back to your Maggie with the promise that you will talk to her about the cave. The ancestors are with us tonight," he said, pointing to the approaching storm. "You know what must be done."

Ben looked out at the dark clouds creeping towards them. "You don't care much for Maggie, do you?" he questioned with caution. Again, he didn't want to start an argument with the old man.

"You say that because you are young and don't take the time to listen. Do you remember our conversation the other day? Maggie is the deer I spoke of in my vision. She has come onto your path and you have strayed from your original path, just like I said you would. Maggie has a great spirit, I can see it in her eyes. I see how it affects you and it is nice to see you happy, but you are at the crossroad. Our ancestors and the cave are on one path, and fame in their world is on the other. I ask you again, where is your heart, young one? You must realize that the road you choose can be traveled by two."

"And you have seen this, Grandpa?"

"I have, Sahale."

"Well, I should get back," Ben said, standing up. "She's going to be mad as hell."

John stood with his grandson. "She will get over it. I made some more tea for her. Will you take it to her for me?"

Ben smiled. "When did you do that? We just got here?"

"I made it before we left the other day. I knew that she would need more."

"Of course you did, Grandpa. She is quite fond of your tea, you know. This will make her happy."

"She is falling in love with you, Sahale, you know that?" John questioned, making his way inside the house. He returned moments later with a thermos in hand and gave it to Ben.

"I think I love her already, Grandpa. I don't want to lose her."

John's eyes softened, putting his hand on Ben's shoulder. "You will not lose her. You must remember that anything worth having usually does not come easy. She might get angry. It is her nature, but she will come around. If she cares for you the way I think she does, then she will do what we ask. Your feelings will be hers. Now go. You have to drive through this storm. You bring her by for a visit when this is all over, okay?"

Ben agreed and headed out into the approaching storm. Maggie was waiting, and for better or for worse, so was the secret of his ancestors.

Chapter 23

By the time Ben reached the Inn, the worst of the storm had passed. Parking his truck, he looked up and noticed a light still on in her room. She's waiting up for me, he thought with a sigh. Crossing the wet street, he thought about just going to his room and avoiding her altogether, but he knew that no good would come of that. Besides, he didn't want to pass up the chance to hold her again. Having Maggie in his arms was becoming second nature to him. It was like she was made to fit the curve of his arm. He walked through the front doors and into the dimly lit lobby. Troy still sat at the front desk, lost in a book.

"It's a bit late for you, Troy, isn't it?" he questioned.

Troy met Ben's glance through his wire-rimmed glasses. "Thank goodness you're back, Sahale," he said with concern. "Maggie came down about a half hour ago. Said her head hurt a bit. Wanted to know if she could get some herbal tea."

"Where is she? Is she okay? Did you call Collin?" Ben asked with alarm.

"I made her a cup of tea and she took it back upstairs. She asked me not to wake Collin. Said she would just wait up for you. She looks tired, Sahale. She needs to rest, I think."

"I'll see to her, Troy. Thanks for looking out for her," Ben said, heading up the stairs. He took them two at a time, racing to her room. He knew she had pushed things this afternoon. He was not letting her go back out tomorrow until she had rested sufficiently, even if he had to take her over his knee. He pulled the key out of his pocket, opened the door, and went in.

"Ahawi," he called, almost in a panic. Rounding the corner, he found her sitting on the sofa watching T.V. "Troy said that your head hurt again. Are you all right?" he questioned, kneeling down in front of her.

She met his gaze with warm green eyes and a weary smile. "It hurts a little. I think it is a legitimate headache. I have managed to work myself up tonight."

Ben took the thermos and poured her a cup of tea. "Grandfather sent some more tea."

"Remind me to thank him," she said, taking the cup from his hand.

Ben stood up and kicked his shoes off before he unbuttoned his shirt. He sat down next to her and pulled her close to him. "Why are you so worked up tonight?" he asked, kissing her hair.

Maggie smiled, running her hand under his shirt. His skin was warm and touching him had become a source of comfort for her. She felt more at ease. A cool breeze blew in from the open window and all seemed to be right now that he was holding her. "What's bothering you?" he questioned again.

She took a deep breath, not sure if she wanted to broach the subject. The truth was, she was just glad he had come back. "It's nothing, really," she whispered, leaning further into him.

"Well, if it's nothing, then why are you anxious?"

Maggie sat up and met his eyes. "You seemed distant at dinner tonight and I think I know why."

Ben brought a finger to his lips and tried not to smile. There was no way that she could possibly know why. This should be interesting. He reached out and brushed a curl off of her face. Is there any light that she doesn't look good in? he wondered not for the first time. Her auburn hair hung in lose curls over her bare shoulders. Her sun-kissed skin seemed to glow from within, making her green eyes shine. If he stared at her much longer, there would be no discussion. He was fighting a strong urge to pick her up and take her to bed.

"You know, you have been here ten whole minutes and you haven't kissed me yet," she said with a smile.

"Well, let me remedy that." He leaned in, kissing her gently. Her lips tasted sweet, and he felt desire run through him. He pressed his lips to hers once more and then pulled back before he lost control. "Now tell me what's bothering you and drink your tea, please."

Maggie brought the cup to her lips and took a sip, savoring the taste of the tea. It was amazing how good this stuff made her feel.

"Grandfather will be pleased that you like the tea so much."

"Really? Because he's why I thought you were distant tonight," she began, looking down. "He doesn't like the fact that we're involved, does he? He doesn't like me."

Ben reached for her hand, sensing how vulnerable she felt. "That is not true, darlin'. He told me tonight that he sees a great spirit in you. He said that it was good to see me happy."

Maggie looked surprised. "But he seemed so irritated tonight. Not wanting to talk about the writings. I just assumed that it was because of us."

Ben took a deep breath. It was now or never. He knew what he had to do. Thoughts raced through his head, he really didn't know where to begin. "He's very fond of you. He asked me to bring you by for a visit when this is all done."

"He's not going to help us?"

"I'm afraid not. I need to talk to you about something."

Maggie set her cup down and crawled onto his lap. "What is it? Is he not happy with the way we're handling the dig? I will do whatever we need to, to ensure the elders' happiness. He just needs to tell me what to do."

Ben slipped his arms around her waist, trying to figure out exactly how to say what he had to say. There really was no good way to say it. "Maggie, my grandfather, the elders, the council, they all want you to stop the dig and close the cave. It has been undisturbed for centuries and they would like it to stay that way."

Maggie looked stunned. "But why? I promise to treat the artifacts with respect. Think about how much we will learn about your people, Ben. We could share that knowledge with everyone. Your people have been so misunderstood. We could change that!"

Ben took both of her hands in his, holding them tightly. "You have done nothing wrong, Maggie. You must believe that. What you found is a very sacred place to the elders. They do not want it disturbed. You have to understand, darlin'. I am torn on this. I cannot turn my back on my people, but I do not want to turn my back on you either. My greatest fear is that you will walk away from me for doing this."

Maggie felt anger well up inside her. How on earth did they expect her to turn her back on this discovery? "Ben, I'm not sure I can do this. This is too big."

"Maggie, you have to. The elders are not asking."

She got up and paced the room. How was she going to explain this to everyone? Collin had already sent things to the lab. She did not know how to stop everything that was already in motion. What was more was that she didn't know if she wanted to. Stopping where she stood, she turned to meet his eyes. Her face was flushed and she knew that the blotchiness was slowly creeping up her body. Any minute now, bright red spots would appear on her shoulders. She searched Ben's warm brown eyes, trying to find the answers that she needed.

"Maggie, please," he whispered.

"What if I can't, Ben?"

"You won't do this for me?" he questioned. He stood up, his anger welling.

"I'm just not sure."

"The will of the council means nothing to you? If that is so, then I must mean nothing to you either! What was this, Maggie? Just some fun? A way to pass the time while you were in a small town?" he said in a raised voice.

Maggie felt like he had slapped her. He knew that it wasn't true, but he said it just to hurt her. Now her anger was full blown and she knew her accent would be thick when she spoke. "How dare ya! After everything I have shared, ya know that's not true! I just need to think about this, Ben! Can't ya understand that?"

"Oh, I understand perfectly, Maggie! You need to think about the fate of my people's culture. Grandpa was right; the white man has never understood our way. Why should you be any different?"

"The white man! You put me in that category?" Maggie asked, hurt. "I have spent my whole life trying to understand different cultures."

Ben reached down for his shoes, picking them up. "I'm not asking, Maggie. I'm telling you. The cave is to be sealed off again and that is final. If you persist, I believe the council will go to court." Having said that, he stormed past her towards the door.

Maggie reached for his wrist, catching it in her hand. "Ben, please... Do na' go! We can work this out. There must be some middle ground here."

He turned and met her tentative stare. Her green eyes shone with unshed tears. He'd hurt her and that was something that he never wanted to do. The council would have the final say, though, and he knew he had to stick to his guns. Even if he wanted to back down, he couldn't. The council would make sure of that. "There is no middle ground, Maggie. I wish you thought more of my people. You really surprised me." With that, he turned and left, heading to the sanctuary of his own room.

The door slammed shut and Maggie jumped at the sound of it. She brought her hands to her face and cried. What did I do? This was not the first time that one of her digs had been halted. That had happened several times due to red tape. This should have been no different for her. She dropped to her knees and sat in the middle of the floor, sobbing. This time she cried for the love she was sure she had lost, not for the one that was taken away.

Chapter 24

The sun peeked through mint-colored curtain and fell on the pillow where Ben's head still lay resting at 7 AM. As it warmed his skin his nightmares vanished into his subconscious and one eye opened. The second eye soon followed until he was able to see the alarm clock on the nightstand. He had spent most of the night watching the numbers change minute by minute and had fallen asleep sometime after four. Now his mind began to recall his dreams, in which he walked down a barren and narrow path lined on both sides by his ancestors. He struggled to look at their faces but couldn't, as they turned their backs no matter which direction he headed. "Is this my heart? Have I done the right thing?" he asked, never hearing a reply.

He sat up and looked out across the street. His truck was in an empty parking lot. The others had gone about their work, not bothering to wake him. Ben was hungry, but his hunger gave way to a feeling of loneliness. He walked across the room, pulling back the curtains to confirm his fears. He then sat back on his bed, put his hands to his forehead, and relived the last week in his head, picking apart every sentence that had passed between him and Maggie. When he reached a point of frustration and was satisfied that he had blown another relationship, he got up and got dressed. That's when he found a note had been shoved under his door.

Ben reached for the note anxiously, and then stopped in his tracks. Did he really want to read what it said? He considered the devastation of a Dear John letter, the unlikely possibility of a complete apology, and then realized the truth would be somewhere in between those extremes, and opened it.

It was in Maggie's own hand:

> Ben, I think last night we both said things out of passion for our roots rather than respect for one another. I also hope you see that this might be the most important find of my career and appreciate that. That being said, we are leaving for the site shortly. I genuinely value you and your help if you decide to join us. I really hope you will.

Ben read the note three times in an effort to sort out his feelings, and try to get a better handle on hers. He was uncertain now more than ever about the whole thing, and decided to go off somewhere and think.

On the hill near the cave, Maggie, Bev, and Collin neared the encampment where Ally, Rick, and Ellen had spent the night. As they approached they saw Ellen attempting to start a fire.

"I'll bet you got wet last night!" Maggie yelled.

"Wet? How do you mean?" Ellen asked, standing up and wiping her hands on her jeans.

"We had a storm pass through town. Didn't it rain up here?" Maggie asked, seeing Ben's tent lying flat on the ground. "Where are the others?"

"Oh...oh yeah, yeah it rained. Those two are being lazy butts in your tent. We used it, to sleep in. We all got a good night's sleep and I was going to try to make coffee."

"It's okay," Maggie said. "Glad you kids are alright. Looks like your shirt got torn. Catch it on some briars?"

Ellen pulled her torn shirt to her body in an attempt to hide it from further investigation. "Yeah, I guess I should change."

"Don't go to any trouble on my account," said Collin, smiling but still out of breath from the climb.

"I swear, Maggie, your brother is charming as hell," Ellen chuckled, unzipping the flap of the tent. "Well, look who's up!"

Ally crawled through the flap. She shielded her eyes from the bright sun, moaning, "Hey, guys. What time is it?"

"Almost seven," Maggie said, sitting down and waiting for

Bev to reach them. "I brought some pop-tarts, by the way. College kids still live on them, don't they?"

"Long as they're not the s'mores. I think that made me sick last night."

Ellen laughed and replied, "Yeah, that was it."

"Just let Rick sleep for now," said Maggie, "but when you guys are ready, can you join us in the cave? We're going to need your help."

"Will Ben be joining us later?" Bev asked, wiping the sweat from her brow.

"Not sure," Maggie said, offering no explanation.

"Oh, well could you call him later and ask him if he found us an easier way up here. We're surely going to need to bring more equipment up at some point."

"I don't know if I'll be able to reach him," Maggie said quickly, walking toward the cave entrance and leaving the others.

"Bev, do you think there will be news reporters up here? I mean, this is a really big find, isn't it? My hair must look like crap," Ellen said, putting on a ball cap.

"Oh, eventually, I'm sure. It's a significant find, but our work is just beginning. We really don't know what we've found yet."

"I'm going to join Maggie," Ally commented, swallowing some aspirin and walking through the trees. When she reached the floor of the cave she found Maggie staring out the twelve-foot-wide passageway and out to the highway and river below. She had her arms folded and didn't acknowledge Alley approaching. "It's a beautiful view," Ally said. "My dad plays on that golf course across the river." Maggie was still silent and Ally sensed something wasn't right. She didn't feel as if she could ask, yet it bothered her. "Hey, Maggie, why do you think they made this opening? I mean, it's obviously been carved out, and it's so wide. Is it just for the view?"

"Oh, I'm not sure, Ally. We were throwing around some ideas last night about astrological tracking, but…I'm not sure."

Ally smiled and looked at her, saying, "You know, I was fantasizing last night about the Discovery Channel doing a show on us."

Maggie turned her head and started back into the main room, saying, "That's a nice thought," in a less than excited tone.

"Well, don't you think that's possible? I mean, this seems significant."

Maggie sat on the large stone shelf and shined her light around the room. "Oh yes, and I'm very excited, but..." She paused and gathered her thoughts. It was rare for Maggie to open up to anyone, especially someone she had recently met, but Ally seemed to her to be sensible and mature beyond her years. "Can I confide in you?"

"Of course you can."

"Well then," Maggie said, drawing in a deep breath, "it seems this place is sacred ground to the Cherokee. We have to respect that, but on the other hand, we have to share this with the world. I mean, my theory is the Adena used this facility, maybe developed it, who knows, maybe 4,000 years ago. Now this is a link between those two cultures that is just groundbreaking!"

"Oh, it would be!" said Ally with excitement. "Not to mention the things we can discover about their cultures."

"Then we have a responsibility as scientists here. Wouldn't you agree?"

"Absolutely," said Ally. The two sat silent, a gentle wind whistling through the tunnel and they shined their lights on objects in the room. "But I'm guessing John and Ben have a problem with this?" Maggie didn't answer right away. "Maggie, I hope this doesn't embarrass you, but I think he really likes you."

"I'm not so sure about that, Ally," Maggie claimed. "Sahale strikes me as...someone who can break a heart if he wanted to, but you're right, neither he nor John are happy about this. I'm not sure that's going to make a difference! What we are doing here is saving this cave from blasting! We'll just have to find other resources, and we will!" Maggie seemed irritated, yet her voice quivered, as if afraid. The pain had returned to her heart.

"Maggie, I've been around Ben Adams long enough to know, he's no player. He's incapable of using or hurting anyone." Again, silence fell between the two for a few moments, and then Ally continued, "He's a good guy, really. I don't want to nose into anything that might have happened between you two, but I will say he's smart enough to appreciate what an incredible find this cave is, and what a find you are."

Just then the voices of the others could be heard descending down into the cave. Maggie rose to her feet, wiped the dust from her pants, and said, "Nothing happened between us. Nothing!"

As the others entered the room, Bev placed a bright lantern at its center near the beautiful mosaic, which was now completely uncovered from the dust which had hidden it for centuries. She gently lowered herself to her knees and ran her fingers over the smooth surface, commenting, "I looked at the pictures for hours last night, but they don't do it justice. Magnificent!"

"What's the purpose, Bev?" Collin asked, joining her. "Something like this, created by a culture with no written word. It must mean something."

"You can see something unique here. In the vast majority of ancient drawings there are men, and sometimes women, performing various tasks, but notice here...we see each couple with children. Very unique."

"My theory: what we have here is a daycare center," Rick laughed at his own comment.

"Oh, you're just amusing as hell," said Ellen.

"That's a possibility, Ellen," Bev began. "You see, Native American cultures took great pride in child rearing. In fact, a western tribe had a saying, 'It takes a tribe to raise a child.' This is a good example of why we have to keep open minds."

"Good point, Bev!" Maggie said, unpacking her backpack in a determined manner. Collin had sensed a tension in her voice all morning but had learned over the years to give her space.

"Maggie, have you looked at this much?" Bev asked, pointing to the mosaic.

"No...no I haven't," Maggie said, dropping to her knees beside Bev. "Some of it is mica, coal, turquoise. It seems Adena to me, and they were traders. We'll need to learn all we can about their trade routes, but with the Ohio River, I am sure..."

"No, I mean, look at the picture itself," Bev interrupted.

Maggie studied, running her fingers over the surface. "The first thing that occurs to me is the story seems to run in a circle, with spokes leading to the center of this one group of people who appear to be of importance, judging by their dress, but with no faces. That could mean the one in the center was omnipotent...or maybe... Hmm, maybe this story takes place over many years and the faces change?"

"Yes, my thoughts, too," Bev replied. "If you follow clockwise, that makes sense."

"Here's a man and a woman, then a family, then adults, and so on. All with a connection to the group at the center." Maggie then rose to her feet and continued, "Collin, did you arrange for an analysis of one of the sealed pots? Maybe that will be a clue."

"I found a lab in Charleston that's capable of everything I can think of doing with it. I'm going to drive it there myself tomorrow," Collin said, looking at the mosaic. "It looks like the guys in the center are standing on a mountain."

"No, not a mountain, Collin," answered Bev. "See how uniform, how square it is? It's probably an altar of sorts." Bev gently rubbed her fingers on the mosaic. "Ah, and look...it's marked with a symbol."

Now Rick joined them on the floor. "Wind, water, it's like a wave function. Maybe they were on the river?"

"Maybe something can be heard here?" Ally chimed in.

The six of them talked, throwing ideas around for nearly an hour, before moving on to cataloging items they found in the room. There were few, and so Maggie felt it would be the best utilization of resources if her students were put to work looking in the area outside the cave. Rick concentrated around the large rock that covered the original opening while Ally and Ellen flanked him right and left. It was early afternoon and the hottest part of the day. Ellen had sprayed her legs and arms with nearly a whole can of bug repellant.

"You know that stuff is going to cause you problems if you over use it," Ally warned.

"I can't help it! I'm being eaten alive!" Ellen said, sitting down on the large rock above Rick.

"Do you have any more water?" Ally asked.

"Here," offered Ellen. "Feeling hung over?" she laughed.

"I feel fine. I'm just hot. I'd rather be down with those three in this part of the day. By the way, I'm sorry if I snored last night."

"We didn't notice," Rick said, grinning at Ellen. "I figured Sahale would be here by now. Wonder where he is?"

"Maggie said he was doing something else today," commented Ally, offering no more details.

Had they looked across the river with binoculars, the three

might have seen Ben, in fact. He sat on the bank of the river on the Ohio side, watching his fishing pole for bites and periodically looking at the cliffs that loomed above him on the West Virginia side. He picked up a piece of drift wood, pulled out his knife, and began to whittle while he stared at the rocks where he knew the team would be working. Before long a pile of wood chips covered his feet, there had been no activity on his line, and nothing had occurred to him that might resolve the conflict in his mind. It was now 2 PM and he needed to hear a friendly voice. Taking his cell phone from his pocket, he dialed and listened.

"Hello, this...you have reached me, but I'm not here. Leave a message...beep!"

"Grandpa, it's Ben. Pick up!" There was nothing but dead air. "Grandpa, please, I need to ask you something." There was still no voice from the other end, so he tried the call again.

This time, John answered. "Speak."

"Speak? Who are you, Quentin Tarentino?" Ben asked, bewildered.

"I knew it was you. I been screening my calls. You seem to know when the good shows are on TV. Where are you?"

"I'm sitting here, fishing in the river," Ben answered. "Grandpa, can we talk about the cave?"

"Okay," John replied.

Ben thought this sounded too easy, expecting an argument, but he continued. "Grandpa, I'd like your trust here on this. Please just listen. I know our people have been charged with a very important task in keeping the secrets of the cave, but who's to say that now is not the time to open all this up? I mean, how secret could it be, thousands of years later? What could we possibly have to hide? I mean, give me a clue and maybe we have nothing to be worried about. Do you understand what I'm saying?"

"This Doctor Phil is no big deal in my opinion."

Ben became frustrated. He shook his head, took a deep breath, and asked, "You're watching Doctor Phil? Grandpa, could you just listen to me, please?"

"Okay, I am listening"

"What I'm getting to is that hillside is a state right-of-way. It's going to be blasted and leveled off unless the ground is identified as being of historical significance, so it has to be recorded as such to save it. I understand perfectly the point of view of our people, but I just don't know how that's going to help us in the end. Are you with me so far?"

There was silence for a few seconds, then John spoke, saying, "This man and woman can't get their teen to listen to them, and they expect Doctor Phil to straighten it all out in this hour."

"Grandpa!"

"And that's not even counting commercials. So really, about fifty minutes or so."

"Are you even listening to me?" Ben asked between clinched teeth.

"Yes, I'm listening. Anyway, just like every show, these people sit there whining, he states the obvious, and then they thank him for his guidance like their happiness depended on it. Is that funny or what?"

"Right now, no, I'm not laughing! You know, I called you because you're the one person I always seem to end up looking to, the one person who always makes me feel better. Now can you please listen to me and give me some advice?"

"I thought I just did? You call anytime, Sahale. Nice talkin'."

Ben heard a click and the call ended. He was so mad that he didn't notice his pole was wiggling until it was pulled off its holding branch that he had secured it to and flew into the water. "Shit!" Ben exclaimed, wading up to his shins to retrieve it.

Jerking on the pole, the line snapped and he stood in the river, reeling in what remained. The situation was so disquieting that he had to laugh. He sat on the muddy rocks and removed his boots, pouring mud and water from them. It occurred to him then what his grandfather had been trying to say. No one could decide for him the path he must follow.

Chapter 25

It seemed hotter at 6 PM than it had all day as Maggie returned to the Suburban to retrieve her notebook. The pavement of the parking lot had been dampened by an afternoon thunderstorm and acted like a natural sauna that made her regret going barefoot. The fact was, Maggie needed to be barefoot. Since her arrival at the Inn a few weeks before, she had wanted to walk barefoot in the lush lawn of the courtyard outside and dig her toes into the soft earth. She had wanted to walk the streets of town in the late evening down to the river and watch the traffic on the water. There were so many things she knew she wanted to do, but had not had the time to do them.

"Maggie," said Troy from behind his desk when she entered the lobby, picking a pebble from between her toes. "I was wondering if you could do me a favor. I borrowed this book from Ben sometime back and I was wondering if you could give it back to him. I haven't seen him around this week."

"No, Troy. Neither have I. Not all week." Maggie could not bring herself to reach for the book, nor could she bring herself to tell Troy that he would likely see Ben before she would. After a moment of uncomfortable silence, the cover of the book caught Maggie's eye and she asked, "Buffalo Creek?"

"Yeah, it's where Ben's family lived when he was very young. I guess you could call him a survivor, then, huh?" Finally Maggie took the book from Troy's hands and studied the cover. "I don't know if you're familiar with the story or not, but it's a good book, you might enjoy it too."

Maggie could still not offer an explanation, but clutched the book and asked, "Have you seen Collin this evening?"

"Yes, ma'am, he was headed for the pool area a few minutes ago."

Maggie continued down the hall and through the door to find Collin, eyes closed, head thrown back, and surrounded by the turbulence of hot water. "I can't believe you," Maggie offered, approaching. "Ninety degrees today, ninety percent humidity, and you come back here and get in the hot tub?"

"My muscles will thank me for the effort later tonight. If I can stay awake, that is."

"I intended to lay down for a nap myself, but I might read some before dinner," Maggie said, opening the book.

"You know what you should have done? You should have accepted those kids' invitation and camped out with them tonight on the hill. It would have done you good."

"I know. I do feel bad about that. Those kids worked very hard this week and I need to hang out with them more," Maggie said, thumbing through the book, "but there are more storms in the area, and I have so much work to do."

"So? They might end up getting a little wet, and when have you ever not had a lot of work to do?"

Maggie didn't answer, accepting it as a rhetorical question, but continued reading.

"You know, life is what happens while you are making other plans. One night roasting marshmallows might do you some good."

"It didn't the last time," Maggie said in a lower tone.

"Oh, I almost forgot," Collin said, sitting up and looking directly at his sister. "I was talking to a friend of mine about that mica surface that covers the north wall. It's a very distinctive curvature, you know. Perhaps an ancient hyperbolic equation was used. Wouldn't that be something?"

Maggie looked up, thought for a second, and said, "Yes, It really would be. I just never considered that because of the shape of the cave appearing to be so rounded."

"Well this might be off the wall, but suppose it was used to focus something to some point? You know, like a satellite dish"

"You're right," Maggie laughed. "That's very far off the wall." Her initial response had no more than left her lips than her face drew serious and she said, "Wait, no, not really. You may be onto something, and if I'm not mistaken, it's a full moon tonight!"

"So? If it is, you might never see it. It's not very clear out."

"The moon was a very important entity to ancient societies, you know that," Maggie said, standing up.

"Yes it was. So? You can go to the store, pick up some food or something to surprise those kids with, and be up there well before dark. So go!"

Maggie drew a satisfied smile and said, "I am! Oh, will you and Bev be alright eating without me?"

"Ohhhh..." Collin moaned, shaking his head, "and for God sakes, sister of mine, if you see Ben, make up with him!" he said before his head slipped back down deep into the water.

"Okay, Okay! I'm going!" Maggie said, blowing him a kiss and running out the door.

Maggie showered, changed, then drove to the store and bought as many items as she thought she could easily carry up the hill by herself. By 8 PM she had traversed most of the hill and realized she had bought far too much. She was soaking wet with sweat and taking frequent breaks to catch her breath. When she caught the sight of smoke from a campfire, she also caught her second wind and picked up the pace.

Rick was sharpening sticks while Ellen and Ally watched, sipping beer. "Put some more wood on there, Ally."

"What wood, Rick?" she said, throwing her hands in the air. "You forgot to gather some, didn't you?"

"Rick! You didn't get wood?" Ellen said sharply.

"Yeah, I'll bet he has that problem, Ellen," Ally said, catching a glimpse of Maggie coming up the path. "Maggie!"

All three ran to meet her and took the bags from her hands. "Hey," Maggie, catching her breath, "can I join you guys tonight?"

"We'll even let you sleep in your own tent!" said Rick.

"Whose tent is that?" asked Maggie, pointing to one that did not look properly set up.

"That's mine. I know, it sucks," said Rick.

"It's not the worst I've seen," offered Maggie.

Ellen placed the bags on the table that was now covered with a tarp, saying, "The Beast! You brought a 12-pack of the Beast! God bless you!"

"Yeah, well, you guys are over 21, and I remembered someone left a can in my tent!" she said, looking at Ally with a raised eyebrow. "I also brought some food, not knowing what you had."

"You done good, Maggie!" Ellen replied, unpacking the bags while Maggie sat, still catching her breath.

The four enjoyed the dusk of the evening, the food, and the company. Maggie felt 21 again as she watched the fire, looked for the moon to peek from behind fog and clouds, and told jokes that would have shocked her students. Maggie was inside her tent changing her clothes when she heard the sound of a four-wheeler in the distance.

"That has to be Sahale, himself!" Rick said when the headlights came into clear view and the motor shut off. Ally and Ellen walked to meet him when it was apparent who it was.

Maggie's heart raced with apprehension. She didn't know what to expect, only that she was overwhelmed that he was there. She listened to the others greet him.

"O-si-yo, dude!" Rick called.

"Sahale, you are a sight for sore eyes!" Ellen said, hugging him.

"I thought I'd check up on you guys. I was driving out the ridge and smelled hot dogs cooking so I figured every bear in the area would be converging on you about now."

"Oh now, don't start that crap!" Ally said with a swat to his arm. "I have to sleep up here tonight, you know."

The four of them reached the fire just as Maggie came out of her tent. Ben saw the flames reflecting off her red hair before seeing her face and remembering the night they had spent alone in this same place. As their eyes made contact he could not say a word. He only drank in her vision and felt an excitement he had not known for days.

"Sahale." Maggie smiled, hoping for one in return. It came quickly.

"Ahawi. How are you?" Maggie answered with a cheeriness meant to send a clear message.

"Fine! Care for a Beast?" she asked, offering Ben a can.

"A Beast? You guys making her a hillbilly?" Ben took the can, but didn't open it. He placed it back on the table, saying, "No, I can't stay. My truck is just parked beside the road out there."

"Oh, bullshit!" Rick responded, "like it's not been parked beside the road before!"

"Have a hot dog, Sahale. I cooked them myself!" Ellen said with pride.

"No way! All by yourself?"

"Yep," said Ellen, as if not seeing the joke.

"No, just wanted to check on you all," Ben said, taking a step backward.

"Ben, please...stay for a while. Come on," Maggie said, handing him back his beer. The five took places by the fire and sat there silently for a moment. Finally, Maggie commented, "I think I just saw lightning way down south. Hope it stays down there."

Ben replied, "Oh yeah, there's some storms out there tonight. At least it's cooled the air down. Nice little breeze blowing, too. It's nice out."

Over time, the conversation lost its tension and an hour later everyone was laughing. Ben walked to the cooler for another can of beer and handed Maggie one also. As she took it, Ben saw the reflection of the flames dancing in her eyes. When he touched the soft skin on the back of her hand his heart seemed to melt. He sat down, wondering about the future, just as he had most of the week. A gentle breeze chased everyone around the fire trying to avoid the smoke. Maggie happened to see the moon, partly peeking from behind clouds and fog and hanging over the hills of Ohio, only hours before it would set.

"Oh! There's the moon!" she said, rising to her feet.

"It's beautiful," Ellen commented, not stirring from her position on a blanket beside Rick.

"Who wants to go with me? I want to see something in the cave!" Maggie said excitedly.

"No freakin' way!" yelled Ellen.

"Don't make me get up," said Rick. "I'm too comfortable."

Ally started to get up from her seat, but then said, "Oh...no way! I'm chicken. You go with her, Sahale."

Ben didn't know what to say. Instead, he stood quietly and

watched Maggie grab a flashlight. At the same instant he had decided he wanted to go bad enough to agree, Maggie grabbed his arm, saying, "Come on, or I'm going down alone."

"What's this about the moon?" Ben asked as they walked.

"It's full tonight and I want to see something. It will just take a few minutes, I promise." When they reached the floor of the cave, Maggie looked down the tunnel toward the north and shut her light off. She gave her eyes a few seconds to adjust, but still saw nothing. The room was pitch black, illuminated only by the occasional flash from distant lightning that channeled down the tunnel leading to the cliff outside. "Damn!" She cursed, turning her light back on and sitting on the large stone shelf.

Ben took a seat beside her and asked, "What were you expecting?"

"Oh, I don't know what I was expecting. Just something Collin came up with today."

A gentle breeze blew through the opening of the cave. They sat in silence for a time. Finally, Ben asked, "You been okay?"

Maggie took a deep breath and felt her heart race a little. Was this a sign that he was ready to forgive her? Looking up, she met his gaze and smiled wearily. "Well, truthfully, I've been better."

Concern raced through him and before he knew it, Ben had reached for her hand. Their fingers laced together just as if they had never been apart. "Is it still your head? Maybe we should take you down to Charleston, to the big hospital. Maybe they can figure out what's going on."

Maggie squeezed his hand in an effort to reassure him. "No, it's not my head. I'm actually feeling much better. The bruises are almost gone too."

"Well, that's good to hear. We were all pretty concerned there for a while."

Maggie looked down at her shoes and then out the cave opening again. "I...um..." Ben reached over with his free hand and put a finger under her chin. He gently turned her face to his. When their eyes met, Maggie felt her lips go dry and her pulse quicken. He was so close to her and the truth was, she had missed him terribly and missed the feel of his touch.

As if seized by something, they both blurted out, "I'm sorry."

"No," Maggie began, "it's my fault. I should have considered your feelings more. I never meant to imply that the will of the elders meant nothing to me. Of course I have immense respect for you and your people, Ben. I was just being stubborn, and not thinking clearly, but I am now, and if we don't show this cave to the world, Ray and his team will blast it to oblivion. We have to save it," she pleaded.

"I know that, darlin'. I know it must be saved. I also know that I said some very hurtful things to you and I'm sure there is no way for you to forgive me. I was angry and I'm afraid that's all I can offer in my defense. I'm sorry, Maggie."

Maggie placed her flashlight next to her on the smooth stone shelf and turned to Ben. Smiling, she met his brown eyes with tears. "There's nothing to be sorry for. I'm the one who put my foot in my mouth. Then after you left, I figured there was no way for me to fix things..."

"And did you want to fix things, Maggie? Tell me that this was not just a small town fling. Tell me that the anguish in my heart at not being able to see you was not for nothing."

"Not being able to see you...not being able to talk to you... I've been going crazy. How can you not know how I feel about you, Sahale?"

The cool breeze blew through the cave again, picking up Maggie's auburn curls. They began to float on it, almost as if someone was pulling on them. Ben took a deep breath, the moon finally shining through the hallway and reflecting in Maggie's green eyes. They looked like two deep pools of shining emeralds and Ben was taken aback. He took a deep breath as Maggie began to take on an otherworldly quality. Her sun-kissed skin shone in the moonlight, almost as if lit from within.

"Maybe I know, but maybe I need to hear you say it," he said, taking a deep breath, trying to slow his shallow breathing.

"This thing...between us..." she began, motioning between them, "it happened so fast. I wasn't sure I could handle it. I wasn't sure if I was ready to move Michael out of my heart..."

Ben pressed his fingers to her lips gently, halting her, "I told you that there was room in my heart for you both. You never have to move Michael out of your heart. I actually look forward to getting to know him through you."

"I know," she said softly, "but I'm still afraid. If I give myself to you... If I open my heart again and something happens to you, Ben... It would kill me. I could not go through that again."

"You can't live your life like that, darlin'. Especially you. You go out and experience life every time you work. Running away is not the path for you."

Maggie looked down for a moment, feeling tears again. She met his gaze with glassy green eyes and knew that she had lost control on her accent as well. "I know that now. I know that more than anything I have ever known. I've tried everythin' to steer ya off of my path, and yet ya always find yer way back to it. I have fought with my mind over and over again, and I always come back to the same realization."

"And what is that, Maggie Mae?" Ben questioned, loving the sound of her accent.

Maggie looked surprised. She knew that she hadn't told him her middle name. Ever since Rod Stewart had released his famous song, Maggie had grown to hate her name. "How did ya know that?" she questioned.

The breeze had picked up and was coming through the tunnel, cooling the room. Ben, however, did not feel cool at all. Desire had gripped him when he saw her in the moonlight, and now he found it almost animalistic. He was finding it hard to control himself. "Collin told me. That's what brothers are for, right? They embarrass their sisters every chance they get? He's been coming by every night."

"He has, has he?" Maggie questioned, making a mental note to thank her brother the next time she saw him.

"What is this realization you keep coming to?" Ben questioned with anticipation.

"Don't ya know? I love ya, babe. I love ya and I'm sorry that I hurt ya," she whispered, afraid of what he might say.

Ben reached out and pulled her close. So close that Maggie lost her breath for a moment, returning the embrace.

This is my heart. The thought came to him and he knew that he was making the right decision. Maggie was right. If he did not let her share the cave with the world, Ray's team would destroy it and all knowledge of it would be lost forever. That could not be what his ancestors had wanted. This was the only way to save it, and save their teachings. The dig would have to continue. He knew that Maggie would treat it with respect. Ben felt the weight that had been bearing down on him the whole week lifted off his shoulders. Holding her again and knowing that she felt the same way for him that he felt for her made everything right.

Off in the distance the thunder rolled and was followed by a flash of lightning. The gentle breeze grew a bit stronger.

"I love you too, Ahawi. From the moment I met you..."

"Hey guys!" the voice called from down the tunnel, halting their conversation.

Ben rolled his eyes, pulling Maggie closer to him. "This had better be good!" he hollered back.

"Why, are you two neckin' down there?" Rick called, followed by the girls' laughter. Maggie let out a soft laugh herself and pulled back from Ben's grasp.

"We could be if you weren't nagging us!" Ben hollered back.

"Well, I hate to break up the party then, but there's a storm coming. We put the fire out and we're heading down the mountain. Looks like it might get nasty. You two should think of coming up out of there. That is, if you can tear yourselves away from one another."

"Nice going, Rick!" Ellen said, slapping his arm.

Ben looked at Maggie for a sign that she wanted to leave. She simply shook her head no. Ben smiled and looked up again. "You kids go on. We're going to wait it out right here. Take my four-wheeler if you want, just be careful. No hot-dogging! Maggie and I will hike out later. See you guys back at the Inn."

Laughter was all that could be heard for at least a minute. "Well, you guys have a good time then. I guess we'll see you," Rick said.

"Yes, we'll see you." When no response came, Ben pulled her close again. "Alone at last," he whispered.

Maggie looked up at him, her green eyes shining again. "You were right, Ben."

"About what?" he questioned before he leaned in to kiss her.

Maggie felt her breath quicken when he pulled back. "I came to the land of the rednecks and found something I lost."

Chapter 26

*B*en threw back his head and laughed. The sound filled the room, and Maggie could not help but laugh herself. She reached up and pulled the tie from his hair, letting it spill over his shoulders. The breeze picked up strands of it, and Maggie thought he looked like he was right out of a Native American painting she had seen at the Boston Met. Lightning flashed again, and Maggie felt the breath catch in her throat. He was so beautiful, and here she was, right next to him, touching him. This wonderful man wanted her, and Maggie felt like it had been a lifetime since they had last been together. Her attraction to him was almost overwhelming. Gripped by her desire, she leaned in and kissed him, but it was almost savage, and she lost her breath.

A gust of wind blew in, maintaining a steady flow of fresh air. Maggie reached up, grabbed the collar of Ben's shirt, and pulled as hard as she could. Buttons went flying everywhere as she struggled to slide it down his muscled arms. Ben shared her desire and could not wait to free her from her tank top. He reached down and pulled it up over her head before she was done with his shirt. Maggie let go of it and raised her arms in an effort to help him with her tank top. Ben could see the lace of her bra in the moonlight and he raised a shaking hand to it, tracing the pattern.

Maggie reached for his hand and brought it to her lips. She kissed it, her eyes never leaving Ben's. In the moonlight, her hair looked blood-red, with an almost luminous quality to it. Ben, not believing it was real, reached out and threaded his fingers through it. Pulling her head back, he brought his lips to her neck. He kissed her all the way up the slope of her neck to her lips. Maggie cried out and she parted her lips, welcoming him into her mouth. His tongue probed every recess, almost painfully. Still, Maggie wanted more. She pushed her body into him, arching her back, and feeling as though she was not in control of herself. Her need for him was almost too great.

Ben put his arms around her ribs and pulled her to him, snapping her head back. He reached down and in one motion tore her bra off of her. Maggie felt the breeze brush against her bare skin and it only inflamed her desire. Reaching for her shoulders, Ben arched her back for her and met a nipple with his tongue.

"Ahh!" Maggie cried out. The sensation was a mixture of both pleasure and pain.

Ben was relentless, almost as if possessed by something. He moved to the other nipple and reached up with his other hand to squeeze her breast. Maggie felt molten pleasure begin to rise within her. Pleasure so strong, she thought for sure she would cry out any moment with her release. She dug her nails into his shoulders with a force she did not know she was capable of. Both pleasure and pain shot through Ben.

Their eyes met, and Ben licked his lips. "Get out of these!" he growled, tugging on Maggie's shorts. Quickly, Maggie reached down and unbuttoned her shorts, pulling them down. She kicked her shoes off before she shimmied out of the shorts. Lightning came again, and she swore she could feel the heat of it.

Ben reached down and unbuttoned his jeans, but Maggie could not wait. She pushed his hands out of the way and unzipped them herself, trying to pull them down. Ben halted her, stood up, kicking his boots off, and freed himself from them. Maggie reached for his hand and pulled him back down to the smooth stone shelf, before she straddled his lap. She ground against him in an effort to calm her desire, but it was no use; she would not be sated until he was inside her. Maggie brought her lips to his, reaching down to try and pull his boxers away. She managed to get them back far enough that she could reach inside.

She wrapped her hand around the length of him and Ben

broke the kiss to cry out. Her touch was pure heat running through him. He had never felt this before and he knew that he'd waited long enough. Needing to fill her, to possess her body, he reached down and tore her cotton panties, pulling them off and throwing them to the side.

Maggie felt tears fill her eyes. He raised her slightly. The pleasure was so intense every time the breeze met her skin that she thought she would go mad before he took her. Ben could wait no longer either. Not wanting to be gentle, he pulled her hips down and filled her instantly.

"Yes!" Maggie threw her head back and cried out, grinding against him again. Her nails met his shoulders and small streaks of crimson shined in the moonlight.

"That's it, Maggie... Don't stop! Don't stop!" Ben's voice came out in a low growl.

Maggie thrust against him until sweat beaded down her skin. Ben held her hips with each thrust in an effort to pull her closer. It was no use, they were already as close as two could get, but still he wanted more. He wanted to possess her body forever, to feel this much pleasure and pain for a lifetime.

The sensation had become too much and he felt waves of it wash over him. The thunder rolled right over them and Maggie threw her head back and cried out. Pleasure so intense shot right through her and she shook. Ben cried out with her, feeling the same release. Warm tears rolled down Maggie's cheeks as she rode the wave of pleasure with him. She wrapped her arms around him tightly. They were so close that nothing could fit between them, and it was not close enough. Maggie wanted more, wanted to always feel his body pressed against hers like this. Ben lost his balance, and they both toppled over onto the smooth, cool stone. The fresh scent of rain filled the room as the breeze died down, taking with it the excruciating pleasure. Maggie felt she could breathe once again.

"What the hell was that?" she questioned, still clinging to his body.

Ben, still heaving for air, let out a little laugh. "That was fantastic! That's what that was!" Pulling her closer, he leaned in and kissed her gently.

Maggie smiled and rubbed her nose gently against his.

"Promise me that it will always be like this, Sahale. Promise me that you will love me this way forever."

"Forever, Ahawi. I promise. I love you," he whispered.

"I love you, too."

Later, standing on top of the ridge, looking out over the river, Ben reached for her hand. The storm had come and gone, leaving everything fresh and clean. Bright stars dotted the night sky. They had managed to climb out of the cave and find the camp sight no worse for wear.

"So, I'm here to help. I hope you've made a great find here. Can you handle that?"

Maggie squeezed his hand tightly. "I understand, babe. I can handle it. Will you call Ray in the morning?"

"Yes. He's not going to be very happy. This is going to cause them to re-work their route. Big delays as well."

"Yes, you're probably right. He will be mad, but I can hear your ancestors on the wind and they are happy. Their teachings will be protected."

Ben smiled at her, knowing he had finally found his heart. For years he had felt like something was missing. In a short few weeks, Maggie had walked in and filled that emptiness. He looked up at the night sky, knowing that she was right. He could see the smiles on the faces of the ancestors. He had chosen the right path and he would not have to walk it alone. Leaned in to kiss her, he knew that his deer would be right by his side always.

Chapter 27

*J*ohn stood astride tomato plants, working the hoe into the loose, rich soil. He was unaware of anyone until he heard a voice behind him.

"O-si-yo, eh-doh-da-hv-ge-do-da!" Joseph said from the edge of the garden.

John continued to hoe, saying, "I hope you like tomatoes. I might have overdone it this year."

"Well it's been a good spring for the gardens, father."

"Yeah, weeds included," John continued, chopping into the soil. "Did you bring me the newspaper?"

Joseph took his hat off his head, wiped his brow, and said solemnly, "Yes, I did." He held it up for the old man to see.

John walked out of the garden and took the paper, looking at it and rolling his eyes, saying, "He's got on that ball cap, inside with four ladies present." He then read the headline: "Archaic Culture Revealed".

"Well, they are all dressed casually. Who are the others in the picture?" Joseph asked.

John pointed to the picture and moved left to right, saying, "That's Rick; Ally, that Texas girl; and Maggie. Did you read it?"

"No, I just picked it up. I put your milk in the refrigerator, too. Why don't we go have some coffee and read it?"

Joseph walked with his father into the house, sat down at the kitchen table, and started to read, "Archaic Culture Revealed."

"What does that mean, 'Archaic'?" John interrupted.

"Old, historical, ancient," Joseph replied.

"Okay, I'm sorry. Coffee will be ready in a minute," John said, looking at the picture again. "You know, I never did have my picture on the front of the paper."

Joseph continued:

> "One of the most important archeological finds in the history of the state has forced major changes in the development of Route 2 into a four- lane. A four-mile stretch of road between New Martinsville and Paden City will have to be rerouted..."

"Skip to the cave part," John interrupted.

Joseph looked over his glasses at his father, fingered through the article, and continued.

> "The cave, which is thought to have been utilized by the Adena people more than 4,000 years ago, contained various artifacts such as pottery, jewelry, and tools, and may have been utilized as late as the mid-nineteenth century by the Cherokee. 'It's quite a spectacular find, as well as breathtaking to see,' commented Dr. Macleod. 'We now have a much clearer insight into the lives of the ancients who inhabited West Virginia. Their achievements included utilizing local plants like willow bark and may apples for medicinal purposes, but the most amazing characteristic of the cave is its design. Like many ancient societies, the Adenas utilized advanced mathematics. They seem to have sized and shaped the cave to yield some interesting effects. Prevailing west to east winds across the north face of the cliff outside the cave are channeled inside, creating sound inaudible to the human ear, yet they may well have an effect on those inside.' Dr. Macleod has already been contacted by the Discovery

Channel, which plans to…"

"Is that all they say about the cave?" John again interrupted.

Joseph fingered and read hurriedly. "Yes, yes I think so," he said, handing John the paper. John took a moment to read through the article, and then again looked at the picture on the front and said, "He always takes his cap off when he comes in my house." He then looked Joseph in the eye, pointed with his finger, and said, "Know why? Because he knows better!"

"Has Sahale seen this, I wonder?"

"Probably not," said John with a smile. "He left for Boston with Maggie."

"Oh. Oh! Is the trip business or pleasure?"

"Maybe both." John shrugged. "It is sad sometimes what a redhead can do to a man's spirit. Look at poor Ricky Ricardo! But, he seems happy, and Maggie has a good heart. I think it is good for them to walk the same path together."

"Sahale following a woman away from the summer here? Away from fishing, golf, four-wheeling? Ha! He must be happy then."

"I saw his happiness," John said, nodding. "They are good together, and now this is behind us and we can get back to normal."

"I think we did the best that we could do for our ancestors, father. I'm sorry if our secrets have been betrayed, and do not blame Sahale. He has made us all proud."

John got up from the table and walked to the back door, taking a pinch of tobacco from the counter. He then looked back and said, "The secret of the cave is still ours. We have kept it well."

Joseph looked confused. He got up from the table and followed his father out the back door. "Wait, what secret are you talking about? They figured out the wind's song. Is there more?"

"Oh yes, and it is still a secret we will pass down. You will find out some day, my son."

"Wait!" Joseph said, quickening his pace until he reached his father's side. "I want to know. Someday you will have to tell me, so why not now? Why not tell me now?"

John took the pinch of tobacco and shoved it tight into his cheek. He then placed his hand on his son's shoulder, saying, "Have you ever watched Doctor Phil?"

About the Authors

Anna Patten is a writer, art photographer, and nerdy bookworm living in the Adirondacks of Upstate New York.

Tim LaSure has spent his life in small towns nestled in the hills of West Virginia. His writing has been influenced by many art forms and flavored by the people of Appalachia.